# Toto's Story

## My Amazing Adventures with Dorothy in Oz

WRITTEN BY
**Steve Metzger**

ILLUSTRATED BY
**Susan Szecsi**

To Dani,
Toto Forever!

# Toto's Story

## My Amazing Adventures with Dorothy in Oz

*First English Edition, 2016*

ISBN: 978-0-692-68095-7

Written by Steve Metzger   www.stevemetzgerbooks.com
Illustrated by Susan Szecsi   www.brainmonsters.com
Cover and design: Susan Szecsi

# Acknowledgements

This book is dedicated to my beautiful daughter,
Julia Ilse Novick Metzger.
Special thanks to Nancy Novick, Lois Metzger,
Charles Galioto, Suzanne Julig, and to L. Frank
Baum, the ingenious creator of The Wizard of Oz.

# Contents

# Chapter 1

# Dorothy and Me

As soon as the ball left Dorothy's hand, I was off. Faster and faster I ran after it down the dusty path. One...two...three bounces. I got closer, opened my mouth, and quickly caught it with my teeth!

I turned around and proudly trotted back. Wagging my tail with excitement, I dropped the slippery ball at Dorothy's feet and waited for her to toss it again.

"Just one more time, Toto," Dorothy said, smiling. I knew she didn't mean it. We can play this game all day.

Toto is my name, of course. I'm a dog, a black Cairn terrier.

After a few more throws, Auntie Em waved Dorothy inside. Too bad...I was just getting started.

Dorothy's my best friend. She's a girl...a wonderful girl. One day, when I was just a puppy, she found me on the side of the road. I didn't even have a collar. All I had was my red ball with yellow dots. Dorothy took me home, fed me, and gave me my name. She's been my best friend ever since.

I brought my ball over to the elm tree and lay down on the grass, panting under the hot sun. My tongue was sticking out. I didn't look dignified, but I didn't care.

*Where's Millie?* I wondered. Millie is a Shetland sheepdog. She lives in the farmhouse down the road. When she's here, Dorothy throws my red ball and we both run after it. Sometimes I get there first; sometimes Millie gets there first. It doesn't matter.

But she was nowhere in sight!

Just then, I looked up at the sky. It was dark gray. That seemed unusual for so early in the afternoon. I started chasing a fluttering butterfly and forgot about the sky.

Then I heard Dorothy's voice from the front porch. "Toto! Toto!" she yelled. "Come inside!"

But her voice didn't sound the way it usually did when she wanted me for supper or my bath. She was really upset. I perked up my ears. Something was wrong, but what?

I stopped chasing that silly butterfly — I've never caught one anyway — and looked up at the sky again. It was even darker than before. The wind began to howl and blow harder than I'd ever heard. The leaves were swirling around and around.

Dorothy was waving her arms and calling my name even louder. "Toto! Toto!" Knowing she really meant it, I ran as fast as I could toward the farmhouse. I almost stopped for my red ball, but I decided to keep moving.

I was scared when I got inside, so I hid under Dorothy's bed where I feel safe. I heard Dorothy's Auntie Em and Uncle Henry shouting for her to join them down in the cyclone cellar. *What about me?* I thought.

I could tell Dorothy was scared, too. But she wouldn't leave me. (I told you she was my best friend.) She reached under the bed and brought me out by the scruff of my neck. It didn't even hurt. Just as she was about to carry me down the stairs, the house started to shake...really hard. Dorothy fell, but she held me close to her.

Well, you're not going to believe what happened next. That heavy house spun around three times and went straight up into the air. *Uh-oh!* I thought. *What's going on?* It kept rising and rising. *Goodbye,*

*Auntie Em! Goodbye, Uncle Henry!* They were still in the cellar.

Then Dorothy, as calm as could be, crawled to the middle of the floor and sat down. I was too excited to stay in one place. I broke away and started racing around the room, barking like crazy. I got too close to the open trap door. *Oh, no!*

I was just about to fall through when Dorothy, my brave friend, reached over and −OUCH! − grabbed one of my ears. Yipping with fright, I looked down and saw nothing between the faraway ground and me. It must have been hard to hold on, but Dorothy wouldn't let go. She pulled me back inside.

I looked into her eyes to see if she was angry, but she wasn't. She closed the trap door and held me close. "Oh, Toto," she said. "Thank goodness you're safe. I don't know what I'd do without you." Believe me, I felt the same way.

That was a thrilling moment, but my amazing adventures with Dorothy had only just begun.

# Chapter 2

# Up, Up, and Away!

The house kept going up, up, UP! We had no idea
where that crazy wind was taking us. I was sitting on

the wooden floor next to Dorothy, who was petting me. That helped me relax a little.

I looked out the window and saw that the sky was still dark. Something whizzed by the front window. It was a tree! Then we saw Uncle Henry's tractor. I had never seen Dorothy's eyes open so wide. "We're inside a twister," she explained. "There's nothing we can do but wait."

A few minutes passed, and we were still going higher. The house began to gently rock back-and-forth. Dorothy seemed to be getting tired. Who could blame her after all she'd been through? She teeter-tottered to her bed and lay down.

I followed her, of course. Before I knew it, she was fast asleep. Not me! I was wide-awake, wondering what would happen next.

Snuggling next to Dorothy, I heard the whooshing sound of the wind against the windows. Then the house really shook, rattling the pots and pans. We started moving sideways. Oh, how I wished Dorothy would wake up, but I didn't bark. Not me! The wind must have shifted again, because now the house was heading downward. *Uh-oh! Are we going to crash?*

Finally, after what seemed like a very long time...THUMP! We were on the ground. *Whew.* All at once, Dorothy woke up. "What's going on, Toto?" she asked. "Are we still in Kansas?" Of course I didn't know where we were. I just lifted my head, tilted it, and gave her one of my puzzled looks. Sometimes I wish I could tell Dorothy what I'm thinking. I was just happy we were both alive.

Dorothy jumped out of bed and raced to the front door with me trailing close behind. Stepping outside, we couldn't believe our eyes!

# Land of the Munchkins

The sky was no longer dark. As a matter of fact, it was the brightest blue I had ever seen. There were just a few puffy clouds, but they were pink, not white. Without saying a word, Dorothy and I gazed at our new surroundings.

I could tell this wasn't Kansas. Some of the trees had rainbow-colored leaves. Red-and-blue birds magically turned invisible as they flew toward us. Let me tell you! I've never seen birds like that before!

"Is this a dream?" Dorothy asked. It certainly felt like one, but I knew it wasn't. We were definitely awake.

And those flowers! There must have been thousands of them. Being a dog, I don't see colors that well. But the brightness of those yellow and blue blossoms made it easy for me to appreciate how beautiful they were.

I *do*, however, have a great sense of smell. And that sweet fragrance was irresistible; I raced from flower to flower, sniffing each one.

"Stop, Toto!" Dorothy exclaimed. "We've got to figure out where we are!"

Dorothy was right. (She usually is.) After one last sniff, I scampered to her side.

My ears perked up when I heard a jingling sound in the distance. Three old men – all dressed in blue − were walking toward us. The sounds they made were getting louder. That was because they had small bells on their round, pointy hats.

I began to bark. Not too loud...just loud enough for them to know I was around. I wanted those guys to know I was ready to protect Dorothy if there was any trouble.

"No, Toto!" Dorothy said. "Don't be rude!"

A woman joined us. She looked like a fairy godmother from one of Dorothy's princess books. Her fancy gown was decorated with shiny stars that sparkled in the sun. She was also wearing a round, pointy hat. But hers was white, not blue.

"That's all right," the woman said. "Your little pet doesn't know us."

LITTLE?!? *Well, I might not be the biggest dog in the world, I thought, but don't call me little!*

"I'm Dorothy from Kansas," Dorothy said, "and this is Toto. Can you tell me where we are?"

"You are in Oz, my dear," the woman said. "This part of Oz is the 'Land of the East,' the home of the Munchkins."

"What are Munchkins?" Dorothy asked.

The woman explained that the people who lived here – including the three men who greeted us – were Munchkins. Gradually, we started seeing more Munchkins walk toward us. Maybe they'd been hiding until they knew we weren't going to hurt them.

I took a closer look. From the youngest child to the oldest adult, the Munchkins were smaller than the people who lived in Kansas. *Hmm...interesting.*

I thought the Munchkins would head straight for Dorothy, but they made a big circle around me instead. One of them pointed at me and said, "What's that?" *Whoa! Are you kidding me?* Then I remembered! We're in Oz now, not Kansas. I might have been the first dog they had ever seen.

I did a couple of simple tricks: standing on my hind legs and rolling over. The Munchkins were very impressed. They clapped and cheered. *Maybe they weren't so bad.*

My appreciation for the Munchkins grew when one of them brought me a bowl filled with water. And I'm sure I was wagging my tail when a girl fed me some tasty snacks. Dorothy had taught me not to accept any food from strangers, but this was different. You can imagine how thirsty and hungry I was!

"Are you a Munchkin, too?" Dorothy asked the woman in the fancy gown.

"No," she said with a smile, "but I am their friend. I am the Witch of the North."

*What?!?* She certainly didn't look like any of the witches I'd seen in Dorothy's storybooks.

"Are you really a witch?" Dorothy asked. "I thought witches were mean and ugly."

"That's not entirely true," she said. "There are good witches and bad witches. I am a good witch."

Dorothy took a few seconds to collect her thoughts. "Since you are a good witch," she said, "please send me home. I'm sure my Auntie Em and Uncle Henry are missing me by now."

"I'm sorry," the Witch of the North said, "I'm not able to do that. But you're a sorceress, aren't you? You can go home anytime you want to."

SORCERESS!?! DOROTHY!?! *I don't think so. She's a wonderful girl, but she can't magically make things happen!*

"I'm not a sorceress!" Dorothy said. "Why are you are calling me that?"

"Look behind you," the Witch of the North said.

Dorothy turned around. "Goodness gracious!" she exclaimed.

# Chapter 4

# The Wicked Witch's Silver Shoes

What a surprise! Two feet with silver sparkling shoes were sticking out from under our house. I trotted over to have a sniff. *Ugh!* They smelled terrible. I raced back to Dorothy.

"That's the Wicked Witch of the East," the Witch of the North said. "As you can see, she's dead. Only a sorceress could have killed such a powerful witch."

"But I'm just an ordinary girl," Dorothy said.

"My house landed on her by accident. I didn't mean to kill anyone!"

"Don't be upset, my child," the Witch of the North said. "Killing the Wicked Witch of the East was the best thing that could have happened. She treated the Munchkins horribly. Now they are free!"

"Hooray for Dorothy!" some of the Munchkins shouted.

*What about me?* I thought. *I was in that house, too! How about, 'Hooray for Toto?'*

A Munchkin boy brought over a small stick, rudely placed it in front of my face, and threw it about twenty feet away. He probably wanted me to retrieve it. *No, thanks.* I wasn't in the mood for any run-and-fetch games. Maybe if he'd had my red ball with yellow dots, things might have been different. But unfortunately for me, that ball was still in Kansas. And so was my friend, Millie. I was starting to miss her.

"Look!" one of the Munchkins cried out, pointing to the bottom of the house. Everyone was startled to see that the Wicked Witch of the East had completely turned into dust. There was nothing left but her silver shoes. I was going to take another sniff, but I changed my mind.

"She was so old," the Witch of the North explained, "that the sun just dried her up." She shook the dust out of the silver shoes and handed them to Dorothy.

"Will these help me get back to Kansas?" Dorothy asked.

"I don't know," the Witch of the North said. "I've heard they possess some kind of magical charm, but I'm not sure what."

"I really want to go home," Dorothy said, starting to cry. I snuggled against her, hoping that would make her feel better. She stroked my fur...just the way I like it.

"Dorothy, I think the Wizard of Oz might be able to help you get back to the land of Kansas," the Witch of the North said.

"Really?" Dorothy said, wiping her eyes. "Who's that? Where does he live?"

Dorothy had many questions about this "Wizard" character. I was too busy eyeing a pair of tiny hummingbirds to listen to everything they talked about. But I did hear this about him:

- He's a wonderful person with magical powers.

- He lives in the Emerald City in the center of Oz.

- You can reach the Emerald City by following the yellow brick road, but there are many dangers along the way.

She also told us about Oz's other two living witches: the Witch of the South (good and wise) and the Witch of the West (evil and powerful). *So many witches!* I thought. I was missing Kansas more and more with each passing moment.

"Will you come with us?" Dorothy asked, desperately. "Please."

"I can't do that," the Witch of the North replied, "but I will give you this." She bent over and kissed Dorothy's forehead. "Nobody will hurt someone who has been kissed by the Witch of the North."

I jumped up to get a closer look at the mark made by the witch's kiss. *It looks like a flower,* I thought. *Pretty cool!*

"Now I must go," the Witch of the North said. "Good luck on your journey."

Then...another surprise! She spun on her left heel three times and vanished. I was startled at her quick departure and loudly barked at the space where she'd been standing.

"That's enough, Toto," Dorothy scolded. "We've got to get ready! Let's find something to eat!" Dorothy was carrying the silver shoes. "You must be hungry, too."

Even though the Munchkins had recently fed me, I was ready for more food. (I have a hearty appetite for a little...er...I mean, medium-sized dog.) I gave Dorothy a friendly "Woof" of thanks and followed her.

It felt funny to be back inside our house. That's because we were in Oz, not Kansas. All the furniture was still there, although a dresser and a couple of chairs had moved across the floor during our wild ride. And, of course, no Auntie Em, Uncle Henry...or Millie.

Dorothy put the silver shoes on a table, went to the cupboard, and buttered a piece of bread. While gazing at the silver shoes, she took a few bites.

*What about me? I thought. Did you forget about your lovable old friend?*

Dorothy must have read my mind because she broke off a small piece for me. *Yum!*

It was time to prepare for our journey. Dorothy found a basket and filled it with bread from the cupboard. After placing a white cloth on top, she changed into her blue-and-white gingham skirt.

Dorothy looked down at her shoes and noticed how tattered they were. "Toto, these just won't do." After hesitating a few seconds, she tried on the silver shoes. "My goodness!" she exclaimed. "They fit perfectly."

Since we were in Oz, I expected something magical to happen. Maybe Dorothy would start to fly...or spin around three times and disappear. But there was nothing at all! *Whew!* We'd had enough excitement for one day.

"Let's go and find that Wizard of Oz!" Dorothy declared. "He'll help us get back to Kansas! I know he will!" Even though I knew nothing about this guy, I gave a half-hearted bark of approval. Dorothy pushed open the door and we were on our way.

There were many roads in the "Land of the East,"

but there was only one paved with yellow bricks. As I said earlier, I don't see colors all that well. So it was up to Dorothy to find it...and of course she did!

# Chapter 5

# A Scarecrow Talks

Since my legs are a bit shorter than Dorothy's, I had to move pretty fast to keep up with her. We walked past some of the houses where the Munchkins lived. They were smaller than the houses I've seen in Kansas. For some reason, all of them were painted blue.

Some of the Munchkins came out of their

homes to bid us farewell. The adult Munchkins bowed and took off their hats. The children waved and cheered.

*We must be famous*, I concluded, *because we killed the Wicked Witch of the East. At least our house did.* I held my head high and strutted along. *No autographs...or paw prints, please.*

As we continued our journey, there were fewer and fewer houses. Then they were all gone, replaced by open meadows and fields. After stopping for a refreshing drink at a sparkly stream, the yellow brick road led us to a cornfield. It was completely surrounded by a wooden fence.

"I'm tired, Toto," Dorothy said. "I need a rest." *I couldn't agree more*, I thought, quickly coming to a stop.

She climbed to the top of the fence, sat down, and stared ahead into the cornfield. A tall Scarecrow stood only a few yards away. He was probably there to protect the corn from pesky crows. At least that's what scarecrows do back in Kansas.

Just like the Munchkins, the Scarecrow was

dressed in blue – from his boots to his floppy hat. To help him stand up straight, a pole had been stuck up his back. *Ouch!* That looked painful! But, of course, he couldn't feel anything.

Well, Dorothy must have been really tired, because she just sat there and stared at him. There were no birds or small animals around to chase, so I looked, too.

All of a sudden, the Scarecrow winked!

"Toto, did you see that?" Dorothy asked, rubbing her eyes in disbelief. "Scarecrows don't wink. I must be mistaken."

I didn't believe it, either. I ran around the scarecrow's pole about ten times, barking like crazy.

"That will be quite enough, Toto," Dorothy said as she climbed down and walked over for a closer look.

Unexpectedly, the Scarecrow cleared his throat and said, "Good afternoon."

"Was that you?" Dorothy asked. "Are you really talking to me?"

"Of course," he replied. "How are you this fine day?"

*Good witches! Bad witches! And now this – a*

*talking Scarecrow! Unbelievable!*

"I'm...er...uh...fine," Dorothy said. "At least I think so." Just to be polite, she asked, "And how are you?"

"Not too well," he replied with a shrug. "Those annoying crows aren't scared of me at all. All they do is eat and eat until their bellies are full."

"Let me help you come down," Dorothy said as she lifted him off the pole. "My, you're very light! That must be because you're made of straw."

I knew Dorothy would help the Scarecrow. That girl has a big heart.

"Thank you so much," the Scarecrow said, stretching his arms and legs.

I trotted over and took a sniff. *I can't help it! I'm a dog! Not surprisingly, he smelled like a bale of hay from Uncle Henry's field.*

Ignoring me, the Scarecrow turned to face Dorothy. "Who are you?" he asked.

"I'm Dorothy from Kansas," she replied. "I'm going to the Emerald City to ask a great and powerful Wizard to help Toto and me go home. Surely you must have heard about the Wizard of Oz."

But the Scarecrow didn't know about the Emerald City or the Wizard of Oz. In fact, he didn't seem to know much at all. "Since I'm stuffed with straw from head to toe," he said, looking down, "I don't have any brains."

*That explains a lot!* I thought.

"I'm so sorry," Dorothy said.

"Can I come with you?" the Scarecrow suddenly asked. "Maybe the Wizard of Oz will give me some brains. I won't be any trouble at all. In fact, I'm very brave. Can I, please?"

Before the words were out of her mouth, I knew what Dorothy would say.

"Of course you can," she answered.

That was the last straw. Oops...sorry about that. Was I mad? You bet I was! I didn't want anyone else joining us. The best team was Dorothy and Toto – not Dorothy, Toto and the Scarecrow! I barked. I growled. I showed my teeth. Pretty scary, huh?

"Don't worry about Toto," Dorothy said. "He barks, but he never bites anyone."

Actually, Dorothy was right about that! I'm

not much of a biter, but I do love to chew things. Sometimes, when Auntie Em gives me a big soup bone. I can gnaw on it for hours. One day, she had an extra one for Millie. She loved it!

"I'm not afraid," the Scarecrow said. "Since I'm made of straw, he can't hurt me." The Scarecrow picked up Dorothy's bag and joined us on the yellow brick road.

*I don't remember inviting you,* I thought. *But I guess my vote doesn't count.*

"I hope you really are brave," she said. "Our journey could be very dangerous."

"I'm only afraid of one thing," the Scarecrow said.

"What's that?" Dorothy asked.

"A lit match," he replied.

# Chapter 6

# My Wild Dream

Dorothy and I were back on the yellow brick road. And...oh, yes, the Scarecrow was with us, too. The farther we travelled from the land of the Munchkins, the worse the road became. Some of the yellow bricks were now missing. Others were cracked.

I didn't really mind the condition of the road. Having four legs, I can climb over jagged rocks with ease. And my paws give me plenty of traction, too.

But, let me tell you about the Scarecrow! With every step, he either stumbled or fell down. He must have fallen about thirty times! I've never seen anyone so clumsy.

Of course, being made of straw, he didn't get hurt. But he definitely slowed us down. *At this rate*, I thought, *we'll never get to see the Wizard of Oz.* How I wished that Dorothy would send him away.

But she just picked him up, patted him on the back, and offered him some encouraging words. "Don't worry, Scarecrow." "That's all right, Scarecrow." "Let me help you, Scarecrow."

And here's another thing. That silly scarecrow didn't even get upset when he fell. He just laughed and said, "Oops," or "Excuse me."

We decided to rest by a brook for some water and food. To my dismay, Dorothy offered to share some of our bread with the Scarecrow.

"Thank you," the Scarecrow said. "But my mouth

is painted on, so I can't eat anything."

I liked hearing that. *More bread for Dorothy and me!*

Dorothy packed up her basket and we got back on the yellow brick road. After a few minutes, we came to a great forest. The sun was beginning to set. In the shadow of the tall, leafy trees, it was getting harder for us to see.

"I'm tired," Dorothy said. "If you see a house where we can spend the night, please let me know."

A few minutes later, the Scarecrow stopped and pointed. "Look!" he called out. "There's a cottage made from logs and branches. Maybe we can stay there?"

*How annoying!* I wanted to be the one who found us a place to sleep. If only the Scarecrow would just go back to his cornfield!

Dorothy knocked on the door, but nobody answered. To make sure it was empty, I barked a couple of times. Silence. We cautiously went inside and looked for a place to sleep. Dorothy found a bed of dry leaves and made herself as comfortable as possible. I lay down next to her.

"Where are you going to sleep?" she asked the Scarecrow.

"I never get tired," he replied, leaning against a wall, "so I'll stand right here and wait for morning to come."

*Not sleeping?!? That's strange!* This guy was really getting on my nerves.

During the night, I had an unsettling dream. It went like this:

### My Dream (by Toto)

*Dorothy and I were back in Kansas. She was throwing my red ball. Millie and I were chasing it... again and again. Then she threw the ball a long way. I was just about to catch it when the ball started to grow. I watched in amazement as it grew to the size of a beach ball. I jumped on top, but it kept on growing. It was now as big as a barn. I tried to hang on, but I lost my balance and fell off.*

Just before I hit the ground in my dream, I woke up. No ball! No Millie! Looking around the cottage, I remembered we were in Oz, not Kansas. It was still nighttime. There was Dorothy, peacefully asleep.

Then I saw the Scarecrow. He was still standing in that very same spot, staring straight ahead. Spooky! It took me at least an hour before I could fall asleep again.

The next morning, I woke up with the sun. Hoping to see some small animals or birds, I jumped through an open window and scampered outside. I chased a couple of chipmunks, which led me to a creek that was hidden behind some trees. I leaned over and slurped down some water. *Ahhh...delicious!*

Dorothy and the Scarecrow joined me. "Toto, look what you found!" she said, cupping the cold water in her hands and drinking it. "You're my hero!"

*Take that, Scarecrow!*

We were just about to continue our journey when I heard the faint sound of someone groaning. *My sense of hearing is extremely powerful, I'm proud to say.* I stood on my hind legs and barked to get Dorothy's attention. She and the Scarecrow stopped and listened. Then they heard it, too.

# Chapter 7

# A Tin Woodman Moves

"I wonder what that is," Dorothy said, slowly walking toward the place where the sound was coming from.

"Since I don't have any brains," the Scarecrow said, following Dorothy and me, "I have no idea."

I wasn't surprised the Scarecrow didn't know what was going on. But, to be honest, I didn't know, either.

After a few more steps, we could see something shining in the sunlight.

Dorothy gasped. I barked. The Scarecrow just stood there.

It was a man completely made of tin...totally frozen in place! *Wow!* He was in the act of chopping down a tree with an axe.

I decided to take action. I nipped at his tin legs. *Ouch!* That wasn't such a good idea. I began to wonder if the Scarecrow wasn't the only one without brains.

"Are you the one making that groaning sound?" Dorothy asked the Tin Woodman.

"Yes," he said in a low, raspy voice. His mouth could barely open.

"How can we help you?" the Scarecrow asked.

"There...is...an...oilcan...in...my...cottage," he whispered. "Please bring it here."

*That was where we just spent the night. No wonder it was empty!*

"I'll find it!" Dorothy exclaimed as she ran toward the cottage.

While waiting for Dorothy to return, the Scarecrow bent over to pet me. I guess he was trying to be my friend. But I was having none of that! I growled and he quickly withdrew his hand.

"Here it is!" Dorothy said. The Tin Woodman helped her find the spots that needed to be oiled: his mouth, neck, arms, and legs.

"Ahhh," he said, lowering his axe and bending his arms and legs. "Now I feel as good as new. Thank you for saving my life."

The Tin Woodman explained how he got caught in a sudden rainstorm about a year before. Since he didn't have his oilcan with him, he became rusted all over and couldn't move.

"Excuse me for asking," Dorothy said, "but why are you made of tin?"

"It's a long story," he replied. "Do you want to hear it?"

*Please say no*, I thought. *Don't we have to go see the Wizard?*

"Of course!" Dorothy said as she and the Scarecrow sat down on a log. I positioned myself on the ground between the two of them.

The Tin Woodman's tale probably didn't take more than ten minutes, but it seemed to go on forever. When I'm listening to long stories like this one, my mind tends to wander...especially if there are birds or squirrels nearby. Please forgive me if I've forgotten any of the details.

### The Sad Story of the Tin Woodman
### (as remembered by Toto)

A long time ago, the Tin Woodman was a real boy. He grew up and fell in love with a beautiful Munchkin woman. The two of them planned to get married. The problem was that the Munchkin woman lived with a mean old lady who didn't want her to leave. To stop the wedding, she made a deal with the Wicked Witch of the East. (That's the witch Dorothy and I killed... remember?) Anyway, the mean old lady agreed to give the Wicked Witch two sheep and a cow if she prevented the wedding. (Pretty good deal, huh?) And that's just what the witch did — she turned him into a person made entirely of tin! He stopped loving the Munchkin woman because he no longer had a heart. So, of course, the wedding was off! To make himself a home, the Tin Woodman cut down a bunch of trees in this forest. And that's where he has lived ever since. The end.

"That's so sad," Dorothy said, when the Tin Woodman finished telling his tale.

The Tin Woodman slowly nodded, then turned to Dorothy and asked, "Where are the three of you going?"

"To the Emerald City to see the Wizard," she replied.

"Why do you want to see the great and powerful Wizard of Oz?" he asked. "I heard he has a bad temper."

Don't try to ruin our plans, I thought. I gave him one of my quieter growls. Grrr!

"Toto and I want to go back home to Kansas,"

Dorothy answered.

Yes, I thought, *Millie must be wondering where I am by now.*

"And I'm hoping the Wizard of Oz gives me some brains," the Scarecrow added.

"It would be so wonderful to have a heart again," the Tin Woodman said. "Perhaps the Wizard of Oz could give me one. Can I come to the Emerald City with you?"

*There are three of us already,* I thought. *And that's one too many!* I could only hope that Dorothy would say no this time.

"Sure!" Dorothy said.

*Good Grief!* Well, there was nothing I could do. And it was time to move on – one, two, three, four of us!

We came to a new part of the yellow brick road that was overgrown with trees. As hard as we tried, we could not get through. The Tin Woodman used his axe to swiftly clear a path. *Maybe it wasn't so bad having him in our group, after all.*

Dorothy opened her basket and took out some bread. After giving me a piece, she ate some, too.

I would have preferred a crunchy dog biscuit, but I haven't seen any of those lately. The Tin Woodman, like the Scarecrow, didn't eat or drink anything. *Hooray!* Before Dorothy covered her basket with the white cloth, I peeked inside.

*Uh-oh! Almost empty!*

# Chapter 8

# A Lion Attacks!

We continued on the yellow brick road. Many of the bricks were now covered with branches and dead leaves. That made it even more difficult for us to make our way.

Every so often, we heard growling noises coming from the forest. I perked up my ears and nervously looked around. I was pretty darn scared.

"Do you think that's a wild animal?" Dorothy asked in a shaky voice. Our travelling companions seemed to be frightened, too.

"I'm not sure," the Scarecrow replied, falling down again, "but it doesn't sound very good."

As we walked farther, I heard more growling. But this time it was my stomach! I was hungry.

"When does this forest end?" Dorothy asked the Tin Woodman. "It seems as though we've been walking forever."

"I don't know," he replied. "I've never travelled to the Emerald City, but my father once told me it was a long and dangerous trip."

Dorothy sighed.

"Don't worry," the Tin Woodman continued. "Nothing can hurt the Scarecrow and me. And you're protected by the Good Witch's kiss." He must have seen the flower on Dorothy's forehead.

"But what about Toto?" Dorothy exclaimed.

*Yeah, Mister Tin! I thought. What about me?*

"If he's in danger, we'll be sure to protect him."

*Good answer!* Of course I didn't hear the Scarecrow say anything about protecting me.

Just then, we heard a terrible roar. In the next instant, a ferocious lion jumped onto the road. I was so startled, I didn't even bark.

With the swipe of his paw, he sent the Scarecrow tumbling to the side of the road. He tried to bite the Tin Woodman's leg but, not surprisingly, he couldn't make a dent. That upset the Lion even more. "Ow!" he cried out.

I was terrified! Who wouldn't be? But to protect Dorothy, I ran toward the Lion, barking like mad! He was just about to sink his sharp teeth into me, when Dorothy rushed forward and slapped his nose. I was amazed at her bravery!

"Don't you dare bite Toto!" she shouted. "He's a helpless little dog...and you're a big, powerful lion!

*You tell him, Dorothy!*

"But I didn't bite him," the Lion whined, rubbing his nose. Then, unbelievably, he started to cry.

"No, but you wanted to!" Dorothy exclaimed. Just then, she noticed his tears. "Why...why...you're nothing but a big coward!"

"Yes, you're right," the Lion sobbed. "I *am* a coward. I have no courage at all. I've always been afraid of everything, including the tigers and bears that live in the forest."

*What a scaredy cat!* I thought. *Oops. I mean scaredy lion!*

Dorothy, that sweet girl, took out her handkerchief and wiped away his tears. We seemed to be out of danger. *Phew!*

"I'm sorry," the Lion said. "Please forgive me."

*Are you kidding me?* I thought.

"All right," Dorothy said, "but you must never do that again."

"I promise," he said, nodding his large head.

Dorothy told the Lion why we were going to see the Wizard of Oz.

"May I come with you?" he asked. "Perhaps the Wizard will give me courage. That would make my life so much better."

I knew Dorothy would say no this time. After all, he just attacked us!

"Of course!" Dorothy replied instantly. "You'll help keep the other wild animals away from us."

*I give up!* Actually, I thought Dorothy's decision made sense. So, now there were five of us walking to the Emerald City. (I'm glad I know how to count.)

At first, I kept my distance from the Lion. Every time I peeked over at him, however, I could see he was a pretty friendly fellow. He even gave that silly Scarecrow a ride on his back.

A few minutes later, I bravely left Dorothy's side so that I could trot beside the Lion. He turned to me and called out, "Hi, little buddy!"

I was ready to be annoyed by the "little buddy" comment, but coming from the King of the Jungle, it was okay.

We happily bounced along, side-by-side. Then the Lion mentioned he was getting hungry and wished he had something to eat. *Uh-oh,* I thought. *Don't look at me, big guy!*

I noticed that the sun was starting to go

down. And it was getting chilly, too! Despite all my fur, I began to shiver. I wasn't in such a cheerful mood anymore.

I looked left. I looked right. There were no houses anywhere in sight. Where would we sleep? How would we stay warm? How would I stay warm?

With every step, the sky grew darker and darker. After a few minutes, we could hardly see where we were going. That made it even more difficult for that clumsy Scarecrow to stay on his feet.

"We need to stop," Dorothy said. She pointed to a clearing next to some large trees by the side of the road. "Since there are no houses around, we'll just have to sleep over there."

Thank goodness for the Tin Woodman and his axe! He chopped down a few trees and made a big pile of wood. Dorothy, who can do so many things, built a wonderful fire. Everyone sat close to it, except the Scarecrow...of course.

As we warmed up, Dorothy and I ate the last pieces of bread.

Just then, the Scarecrow did something that

helped us. (*Yes, it was a surprise to me, too!*) Instead of leaning against a tree and staring into space, he gathered nuts and filled Dorothy's basket with them. Even though nuts aren't my favorite food, this was no time to be picky.

Later on, when it was time to sleep, the Scarecrow placed some dry leaves on top of Dorothy to keep her warm. That was considerate, too. But since I was right next to her, he put those leaves all over me, too. They felt scratchy, so I shook most of them off.

Before closing my eyes, I looked up at the night sky. *Wow!* There must have been a million stars. And there was a big, full moon. It reminded me of warm summer nights on the front porch with Dorothy, Auntie Em, and Uncle Henry. Sometimes Millie was there, too. I really felt homesick. I lifted my head and howled, "Awoooo! Awoooo!"

"Shhh!" Dorothy said. After one more "Awoooo!" I stopped. A few minutes later, I was fast asleep.

The next morning, I felt a bit itchy. It might have been from those leaves the Scarecrow threw on me. I flipped myself over and rubbed my back on the rough grass, back-and-forth, back-and-forth. *Ooh...ahhh...ooh...ahhh.* It felt wonderful.

I guess I was putting on quite a show because everyone was watching me. I immediately hopped up on my four legs, and stared back until they all looked away.

Dorothy walked over to a large, nearby lake and washed her face. Silently I followed her and took a drink. *Mmm.*

Suddenly, that lake became irresistibly inviting. Without thinking, I dashed right in. (Did I tell you I was a good swimmer? I am!) The water was cool and very refreshing! Keeping my head above water, I started doing the dog paddle (yes, the dog paddle!) toward the center of the lake.

All of a sudden, I saw something swimming near me. It had the head of a dragon and a long scaly neck. It looked like something from Dorothy's book about mythological creatures. It was...it had to be...a SEA SERPENT! *Whaaaaat?* Let me tell you...I've never been so scared!

Immediately I turned around and swam as fast

as I could to the shore. Breathing heavily, I finally made it! I faced the lake and loudly barked to let the others know what I just saw. After staring at the lake for a few moments, they looked at me with puzzled expressions. Nobody could tell why I was making such a big racket. That's because the sea serpent was gone.

*I give up,* I thought, briskly shaking the water off my body.

"Toto, be careful!" Dorothy exclaimed. "You're going to splash the Tin Woodman! That won't be good."

*Oops...sorry about that.* I moved a few yards away and continued shaking until I was almost dry.

We gathered our belongings and soon we were travelling again. There were fewer trees as we moved along. We finally left the great forest! *Hooray!*

In the afternoon, we came to a wide river. The yellow brick road stopped at the riverbank and picked up again on the other side. I looked straight ahead. To my relief, there didn't seem to be any sea serpents.

"How will we get across?" Dorothy asked in a troubled voice.

"That's easy," the Scarecrow replied. "The Tin

Woodman will build us a raft. Then we can float over to the other side."

*For someone without any brains*, I thought, *that's a pretty good idea!*

The Tin Woodman began chopping down trees. While we waited, I lay down by Dorothy's side, my head in her lap. She told me how much she missed Auntie Em and Uncle Henry.

That reminded me of Millie. I remembered the times we jumped in big piles of leaves in the fall and swam in the blue lake during the summer.

After the Tin Woodman fastened the logs together, the raft was finished. With help from the Scarecrow and the Lion, he proudly placed it in the water.

Holding me in her arms, Dorothy stepped onto the raft and carefully sat down. The Lion almost tipped it over when he jumped on board, but the Scarecrow and the Tin Woodman quickly stood on the opposite end of the raft to keep it balanced.

Then we were off! The Tin Woodman and the Scarecrow used long wooden poles to push the raft along. *Good work, guys!*

When we were halfway there, a swift current began carrying us downstream. *Yikes!* The yellow brick road was no longer in sight.

"This is bad!" the Tin Woodman exclaimed. "We're being carried away to the land of the Winkies! That's where the Wicked Witch of the West lives!"

"If that happens," the Scarecrow said, "I won't get my brains."

"And I won't get my courage," the Lion said.

"And I won't get my heart," the Tin Woodman said.

"And I won't get back to Kansas," Dorothy said.

*And I won't see Millie,* I thought.

Just when it seemed things couldn't get worse, they did! The Scarecrow tried to stop the raft by pushing his pole deep into the muddy bottom of the river. But the raft didn't stop...it kept right on going. And...I couldn't believe my eyes...the Scarecrow was still holding on to his pole!

I know I've had my problems with the Scarecrow, but I didn't want anything bad like this to happen to him.

"If I only had some brains," the Scarecrow called out, "then I could think my way out of this mess!"

With tears in her eyes, Dorothy waved goodbye.

# Chapter 9

# A Stork Saves the Day!

As our raft rushed downstream, we looked back at the Scarecrow. He was getting smaller and smaller in the distance.

"I hope he's not gone forever," Dorothy whispered.

The Tin Woodman was so sad that he began to cry.

"Please don't do that," Dorothy said in her most comforting voice. "You might rust."

"You're right!" he said, stopping at once.

"We've got to do something!" the Lion roared. "I'll swim to the shore and pull the raft behind me. Just hold on to the tip of my tail and don't let go!"

Quick as a wink, he dove into the water. The Tin Woodman grabbed his tail and held on tight.

*Go, Lion, go! Go, Lion, go!*

The Lion's courageous actions reminded me of the time I barked at a coyote back in Kansas. Auntie Em told everyone I was very brave.

It was hard work for the Lion to swim against the current, but he finally pulled us to the other side.

"We've drifted so far from the Scarecrow," Dorothy said as she stepped onto the shore and turned around. "I can't see him at all!"

"Let's walk back toward the yellow brick road," the Tin Woodman suggested. "We'll be sure to see him when we get closer."

The four of us hiked and hiked until...

"There he is!" the Lion roared.

*He looks so sad and lonely in the middle of the river,* I thought. Yes, I actually felt sorry for Mr. Straw.

"What can we do to save him?" Dorothy asked.

The Tin Woodman and the Lion both shook their heads. I whimpered a little. No one, including Dorothy, had any solutions.

At that moment, a big white bird flew overhead. It was a stork! She saw our funny little group and landed next to us.

"Where are you going?" the Stork asked.

At first, I was surprised to hear a talking stork. But then I looked around and remembered that lions and scarecrows – even a Tin Woodman – talked in the Land of Oz.

Dorothy told the Stork about our journey to the Emerald City. "But we won't leave this spot," she continued, "until our friend is back with us." She pointed to the Scarecrow in the middle of the river.

"I wish I could help you," the Stork said, glancing at the Scarecrow, "but he looks too heavy for me to carry. I guess I'll be on my way."

"Don't go!" Dorothy pleaded. "He's only made of straw, so he hardly weighs anything at all."

"Well, I'll give it a try," the Stork said. "But if I can't carry him, I'll have to drop him in the water."

The Stork flapped her wings and flew toward the Scarecrow. She tried to snag him with her great claws...but missed. Again and again she tried. Finally, the Stork was able to grasp one of the Scarecrow's arms, lift him off the pole, and carry him to the shore.

"Welcome back, Scarecrow!" the Tin Woodman yelled.

The Lion roared, Dorothy clapped her hands, and I yipped with delight.

The Scarecrow was so happy he hugged everyone...even me! (It felt scratchy, but not too bad.)

"I was afraid I was going to be there for a long, long time," he said.

"That was very kind of you," Dorothy said to the Stork. "How can we thank you?"

"I'm just glad I could help out," the Stork replied as she flew away. "Bye-bye."

I watched the Stork until she was just a tiny dot. Then she was gone.

Since we had drifted so far downstream, we still had a long walk to reach the yellow brick road.

Dorothy pointed to a small patch of scarlet flowers. "They're the brightest red I've ever seen!" she exclaimed.

I stopped to sniff a few. Curiously, they didn't smell like anything at all.

"Watch out for those," the Tin Woodman warned.

"Why?" Dorothy asked.

"They're poppies," he replied. "When many of them grow close together, anyone who breathes their fumes will fall into a deep sleep...forever."

"My goodness!" Dorothy cried. "But there aren't that many here, so I guess we're safe."

As we continued, however, we came across a large field that was completely covered by those dangerous poppies.

"I need to rest," Dorothy said, slowing down. "I'm soooo tired."

"It's not safe to stop!" the Tin Woodman called

out. "Keep walking!"

"I just can't," Dorothy said as she lay down among them. In a few seconds, she was fast asleep.

*Oh, no!* I thought, nudging her arm with my wet nose. *Wake up!*

Just then, my eyes began to close. too.

"What should we do?" the Scarecrow asked. "We've got to get her back to the yellow brick road! If we leave her here, she'll sleep forever."

The Lion was no help, either. His eyelids drooped as he curled up on the ground.

The only ones not getting tired were the Scarecrow and the Tin Woodman. *I guess that made sense.*

"Don't fall asleep!" the Tin Woodman yelled, shaking the Lion. "Get away from the poppies as fast as you can! The Scarecrow and I will take care of Dorothy and Toto! But if you fall asleep, we won't be able to carry you. You're too heavy!"

Even though the Lion was extremely tired, he slowly rose and bounded away from us in the direction of the yellow brick road.

I was too exhausted to do anything but snuggle against Dorothy. I must have fallen asleep right away, because I don't remember anything after that.

While I slept, I dreamed about Auntie Em petting me by the fireplace on a wintry night, my red ball tucked under my paw. When I woke up, I was surprised to see that all of us were no longer in the field of poppies. We were on a patch of grass not far from the yellow brick road.

"How did we get here?" Dorothy asked, rubbing her eyes.

The Scarecrow explained that he and the Tin Woodman carried Dorothy and me away from the poppies. When they got to a bend in the river, they discovered the Lion, who was fast asleep.

Since they weren't able to carry the Lion with Dorothy and me, they had to go back for him after dropping us off. When they returned, they tried to pick him up, but couldn't. Then the Tin Woodman had a brilliant plan!

He cut down a tree and made a rolling cart from its branches and trunk. The Scarecrow and the Tin

Woodman lifted the Lion into the cart. Using all their strength, they pushed the cart away from the poppies.

*Whew! What an adventure!*

"Thank you for saving Toto and me...and the Lion," Dorothy said to the Scarecrow and the Tin Woodman.

"Yes!" the Lion said. "I'd have slept forever if you hadn't rescued me."

I expressed my gratitude by barking three times and wagging my tail as fast as I could.

"It's getting late!" Dorothy said, gazing at the sky. "Let's go!" Soon we were back on the yellow brick road.

"We're getting close to the Wizard," she said, looking toward the Emerald City, "and he'll give us everything we want. I just know it!"

Dorothy was so hopeful, I really wanted to believe her. But, truthfully, I didn't know what to think.

# Chapter 10

# I Make a New Friend

I took a few steps and hopped on the Lion's back. By looking up and nodding, he showed me that he didn't mind.

*I'm the Prince of the Jungle!* I thought, holding my furry head high.

The road was in good shape in this part of Oz. Since there were no missing bricks, the Scarecrow was better able to keep his balance and not fall down so much. *Thank goodness!*

We passed some houses along the way. They were green, not blue, like the ones where the Munchkins lived.

Some people came out to greet us, but when they saw the Lion, they quickly went back inside and locked their doors. *Come on!* I wanted to say. *He's friendly.*

"I'm getting hungry," Dorothy said. "And Toto must be starving. He hasn't had a proper meal in days." *You said it!* I jumped off the Lion and sprinted to her side, waiting for her to pet me. She did.

"Not only that, we also need a place to sleep," Dorothy said as she looked up at the darkening sky. She marched to one of the larger farmhouses and knocked on the front door.

An elderly woman with a kind face partly opened the door. "Can I help you?" she asked.

"Hello, my name is Dorothy and I'm from Kansas," Dorothy replied in a cheery voice. "These are my friends. We're very hungry and we have no place to sleep."

"I'm Catherine," the elderly woman said. She opened the door a little wider. "Oh, dear! There's a lion with you!"

"Yes," Dorothy said, "but he's a cowardly lion. He's more afraid of you than you are of him."

I wasn't too sure about that, especially when I saw the concerned look on Catherine's face. But the flower on Dorothy's forehead seemed to reassure her. "I see you've been kissed by the Witch of the North," she said. "Please come in...all of you."

"Oh," Dorothy said, touching her forehead. "I had almost forgotten about it."

I sniffed here and there. That's what I usually do when I find myself in a new place. The wood-burning fireplace in Catherine's house smelled a lot like the one in Dorothy's home in Kansas. That was comforting. But it also made me feel a little homesick.

Then I noticed a bowl filled with water on the floor. *Hmm*, I thought. *What other animal lives here? Maybe it's a dog.* I didn't see or hear anything. I was confused. I barked once.

"Shhh, Toto!" Dorothy said. "Don't be rude.

We're guests here."

Catherine chuckled. "Toto must be curious about that water bowl," she said. "It belongs to Missy Boots, my kitten. She's only six months old... and very shy."

"I didn't know there were any cats in Oz," Dorothy said.

"Just a few," Catherine said. "There are some inside the Emerald City and some here in the countryside. I'm lucky to have one."

"Are we close to the Emerald City?" the Tin Woodman asked.

"Not too far," Catherine replied. "If you start early tomorrow morning, you should be there by afternoon."

"Soon we'll see the Wizard!" the Scarecrow exclaimed.

"Then we'll get our wishes granted!" added the Tin Woodman.

*And Dorothy and I will be back in Kansas!* I thought.

"Let's talk more later," Catherine said, "but right now I'm going to make hot suppers for all of you."

I lay down on the floor and waited. Where was that kitten? Out of the corner of my eye, I saw something move. It must have been Missy Boots. *What a name!* I thought. *It certainly isn't as dignified as Toto.*

Then I saw a little black head peeking around the corner. Like a tiny tiger, she slowly made her way toward me. Not wanting to scare her, I tried to remain perfectly still. (My tail might have been wagging a little, but I couldn't tell.)

When she was right next to me, she tapped my leg with her little paw. It didn't hurt at all. I lifted my head and she ran behind a chair. A few seconds later, she came back and did it again. I guess she was named Missy Boots because she was black with four white paws...just like white boots.

"Don't hurt her, Toto!" Dorothy said, seeing Missy Boots run away.

*I wouldn't dream of hurting Missy Boots,* I thought, feeling some annoyance. *Can't you see we're just playing?*

After a few minutes, she wasn't running away

anymore. She was smacking me all over, especially my tail. Since I usually feel like I'm living in a world of giants, it was nice to play with someone who was smaller than me.

Fooling around with this cute kitty reminded me of Millie. I'm sure she would have enjoyed playing with Missy Boots, too.

"Supper is ready!" Catherine called out from the kitchen. "Please sit down at the table."

Catherine served porridge and rye bread to Dorothy. The lion's meal was porridge, too, but he didn't like it.

"Oats are for horses," he whispered to the Scarecrow, "not lions!"

As usual, the Tin Woodman and the Scarecrow ate nothing at all.

Catherine put a plate of scrambled eggs on the floor, right next to Missy Boots' food dish. I didn't really mind, except I was hoping to eat at the table with Dorothy and everyone else. *Why is the Lion sitting at the table...and not me?* I thought. *We're both animals! Not fair!*

I felt better when I looked down and saw Missy Boots eating some of my food. That was cute! I playfully pushed her head away with my head. She kept right on eating my eggs. She was a tough kitty, that Missy Boots!

Later on, I overheard some of the conversation coming from the table. Dorothy was telling Catherine about our reasons for wanting to see the Wizard.

"The Wizard of Oz is very powerful and mysterious," Catherine said. "Nobody is sure what he looks like. Some people have said he even takes different forms. I've also heard that getting to see him can be difficult."

"But we've come such a long way," the Tin Woodman said, looking downward.

"He'd better see us!" the Lion roared.

"Uh...of course he will," Catherine said with a nervous smile. "Now it's time for everyone to get a good night's sleep." She gave Dorothy a comfortable bed and I lay down by her side. After a few moments, Missy Boots lay next to me. We were a cozy little trio.

The Scarecrow and the Tin Woodman stood

quietly in a corner as the Lion guarded the door.

The next morning, we thanked Catherine for her hospitality and said our goodbyes. I think Missy Boots knew I was leaving. She nuzzled me and I licked the top of her head. *Goodbye, little friend,* I thought. *I hope we meet again someday.*

Back on the yellow brick road, we continued our journey. After a while, we could see a beautiful green glow.

"That must be the Emerald City!" Dorothy called out.

*Chapter 11*

# The Emerald City...at Last!

As we rushed toward our destination, the Scarecrow tripped over me and fell. *Ouch! That hurt!* He didn't even say, "I'm sorry." I thought I was done being annoyed with him, but now I wasn't so sure.

It was afternoon when we finally came to the

end of the yellow brick road. *Hooray! We made it!* A thick green wall with a green gate stood between the Emerald City and us. A guard in a green uniform appeared.

"I am the Keeper of the Gate," he announced gruffly. "Why are you here?"

"We want to see the great Wizard of Oz," Dorothy replied in a steady voice.

The Gatekeeper's eyes opened wide with surprise. "It's been a long time since anyone has asked to see the powerful and terrible Wizard of Oz!" he exclaimed.

*Wait a minute!* I thought. *First, the Witch of the North told us that the Wizard was "wonderful." Then Catherine said he was "mysterious." Now we're hearing that he's "terrible." What's the real story with this guy?*

"If you're here with foolish requests," the Gatekeeper warned, "he might get angry and destroy you all in an instant."

"Maybe we should think this over," I heard the Tin Woodman whisper to the Scarecrow.

"We're not afraid!" Dorothy declared. "We've had a long, hard journey...and we're not turning back!"

"Since you insist on seeing the great Wizard of Oz," the Gatekeeper said, "I will take you to his palace." He opened a fancy box filled with eyeglasses of every shape and size. All of the lenses were made of green glass.

"You must put these on while you're here!" the Gatekeeper commanded.

"Why?" Dorothy asked.

"If you don't," he said, "the brightness of the Emerald City will blind you. Even when you're inside the palace, you must wear them." *What?!? Nothing is easy in the land of Oz,* I thought.

The Gatekeeper dug out a pair of glasses that fit Dorothy perfectly, and he locked them in place.

He also found glasses for the Scarecrow, the Tin Woodman, and the Lion. When it was my turn, he finally came up with a small pair that was the perfect size for me. I wasn't too happy about wearing them. At first, I lost my balance and stumbled around. Then I tried to shake them off. No luck!

My antics must have amused the Scarecrow because he laughed and said, "That's so funny!" I felt like biting him. But I knew he wouldn't feel anything if I did.

*Okay, Scarecrow!* I thought. *No more Mister Nice Dog!*

"It's off to the palace!" the Gatekeeper announced as he swung open the gate.

*We made it!* We were finally inside the Emerald City!

Although my eyes were protected, I was still dazzled by the beauty of this amazing place! The streets were paved with sparkling emeralds and lined with green houses.

"I can't believe it!" the Lion exclaimed.

"This is very different from Kansas!" added Dorothy.

There were many kinds of shops in the street. Everything being sold was green, including candy, popcorn, shoes, lemonade, and hats. *If you don't like the color green,* I thought, *you really shouldn't live here!*

Many women, men, and children were walking

around. Of course, they were all dressed in green. Everyone stared at us. Some children hid behind their mothers when they saw the Lion.

*Perhaps they're really hiding from me*, I thought. *I can look pretty fierce, you know. Grrr.*

Deciding to be sociable, I trotted over to a young boy. I was hoping he would pet me. His mother hurried him away. *How rude!* But we weren't here to make friends, I remembered. We were here to meet the Wizard...and go home!

The Gatekeeper led us through the streets until we came to an enormous building. There were green marble pillars in front, a glass dome on top, and a gigantic stairway that led to the door.

"Magnificent!" Dorothy exclaimed.

"This is the Palace of the Wizard of Oz!" the Gatekeeper declared. "I will leave you now!" In an instant, he was gone.

We climbed the stairs and a soldier with a green uniform met us at the door. "What do you want?" he demanded.

"If you please, sir," Dorothy said, "we have come

to see the great and powerful Wizard of Oz."

"Follow me!" the soldier said as he opened the door. We had to wipe our feet (and paws) on a green mat before we entered a large hall inside the palace. "Now I will go to the Throne Room and give the Wizard your request. Wait here until I return!" He marched off.

"If the Wizard won't see us," Dorothy sighed, "I don't know what I'll do."

After a few minutes, the Lion started pacing from one end of the hall to the other. Suddenly, he stopped and let out a loud roar. I must have jumped about two feet into the air. "I'm sorry," he said, "but I'm not used to being cooped up like this."

"That's all right," Dorothy said, patting him on the back. "I understand."

All of a sudden, the Scarecrow began hopping around. He looked pretty foolish. "This is what I do," he said, "when I need some exercise." Strands of straw fell from his body.

"Stop!" Dorothy cried out. "You're falling apart!"

"It's not a problem," the Scarecrow replied. "I've

got plenty of straw left." He gathered the loose pieces and rolled them into a ball.

"Get ready!" the Scarecrow yelled as he threw a "straw ball" toward the Tin Woodman. But the Tin Woodman couldn't bend his metallic arms fast enough to catch it and the ball fell to the floor.

"Fetch, Toto!" the Scarecrow called out to me. I tilted my head and looked at him as if he was talking nonsense. *Are you kidding me?* I thought.

Finally, the soldier returned.

"What did the Wizard say?" Dorothy asked, excitedly. "Will he see us?"

"When I first mentioned your request, he said I should send you back to where you came from. But after I told him about your silver shoes and the mark on your forehead, he changed his mind."

"That's terrific!" Dorothy said, clapping her hands.

"It will be one of you at a time," the soldier continued, "starting tomorrow." He blew a whistle and a young girl dressed in a green silk gown entered.

"This girl will bring you to your rooms," the soldier said. "All of you can spend the night right here in the palace."

*I hope there's food!* I thought. *I'm really hungry!*

The young girl had green skin, green hair and green eyes. She bowed before Dorothy and said, "Follow me." I knew she wanted me to come, too.

After Dorothy said goodbye to our fellow travellers, we followed the green girl through seven passages and up three flights of stairs until we arrived at our room.

*Quite a palace!* I thought.

Everything was green, of course – green books, green flowers, even a bed with green sheets. I was happy to have some time alone with Dorothy... especially away from that silly Scarecrow!

"Make yourself at home," the green girl said. "I will now bring the other guests to their rooms." Walking toward the door, she continued, "The Wizard will send for you in the morning. Good night."

Just then I smelled something wonderful. I dashed over to a table in the middle of the room and jumped onto a chair. I saw a plate of beef stew... it was steaming hot! Dorothy sat down and shared some with me. *Yum!*

After dinner, Dorothy picked up one of the green books from a bookshelf and began reading it to me. It was a counting book. "One green sun, two green flowers, three green houses..." You get the idea.

Dorothy turned off the light and lay down on top of a big bed. I climbed aboard and curled up near her feet. "I miss sleeping in a comfortable bed like this," she said, closing her eyes. "Soon we'll be back home, Toto."

*I hope so,* I thought, drifting off to dreamland.

The next morning, there was a knock on the door. It was the green girl again. She led us downstairs to the Throne Room. "The Wizard is ready to see you now," she said to Dorothy, "but you must go inside alone."

"I'll be back soon," Dorothy said, looking down at me.

*No way!* I thought. *Dorothy and I are a team! She's not going in there by herself!*

The green girl opened the door and Dorothy stepped inside the Throne Room. But before she could lock me out, I quickly scooted past her.

"You naughty boy," Dorothy said to me, smiling. I knew she wasn't really angry.

We were in a big, round room with a domed ceiling. The walls and the floor were covered with large emeralds. Even with our glasses, I couldn't believe how brightly they sparkled. But where was the Wizard?

# Chapter 12

# The Mysterious Wizard

"I am the great and terrible Wizard of Oz!" a deep voice thundered. We looked at the throne in the middle of the room and couldn't believe our eyes. Above the seat, suspended in mid-air, was a head. No body! No arms! No legs! Just a gigantic hairless head with two eyes, a nose, and a mouth!

We gawked at this unbelievable sight in stunned silence. I had no idea what the Wizard would look like, but I didn't think he would be a big, bald head! I was terrified. I'm pretty sure Dorothy was scared, too.

"Who are you?" the Wizard boomed. "Why do you seek me?"

"My name is Dorothy, your Wizardness," she replied in a timid voice. "I have come to ask you for help."

The unblinking eyes of the Wizard stared directly at us.

"Why did you bring your dog?" he demanded. "I requested that you come alone!"

"Toto is my best friend!" Dorothy said, her voice growing stronger. "Wherever I go, he goes!"

*What a pal!*

"Never mind!" the Wizard said. "Where did you get those silver shoes?"

"I got them from the Wicked Witch of the East," she replied. "My house landed on top of her...and killed her."

"Interesting...and what about that mark on your forehead?" he asked. "Did the Good Witch of the North really kiss you?"

Dorothy nodded.

"What is your wish?" the Wizard asked in a thunderous voice.

"Please send me back to Kansas," Dorothy said. "That's where I live with my Auntie Em and Uncle Henry. I'm sure they're both very worried about me."

The Wizard's eyes rolled around and he blinked three times. "If you want me to use my magic powers to send you home," he said, "you must do something for me first."

"What is it?" Dorothy asked. "I'll do anything."

"Kill the Wicked Witch of the West!" answered the Wizard.

*What!?!?! We've already killed one witch! Isn't that enough?*

"But I can't!" Dorothy exclaimed.

"You killed the Wicked Witch of the East!" the Wizard exclaimed. "There is now only one evil witch left in Oz. When she's dead, I will send you back to Kansas...not before!"

Dorothy was so upset, she began to cry. "I've never killed anything on purpose in my life," she sobbed. "And how could I possibly kill the Wicked Witch of the West? If a powerful Wizard like you can't kill her, how do you expect me to do it?"

*That's right, Mr. Big Shot Wizard! How are you going to answer that one?*

The Wizard closed his eyes as if in deep thought. After a few moments, he spoke again.

"That is your problem to solve," he solemnly replied. "But remember...only when the Wicked Witch is dead will you see your Aunt Em and Uncle Henry again."

"But...but...," Dorothy stammered.

"Now go!" the Wizard bellowed. "And don't come back until you've completed your task!"

*What a grouch!* I thought.

Tearfully, Dorothy walked slowly out of the

Throne Room. Before leaving, I turned around and barked twice at the Wizard's head. His eyes glared at me, but he said nothing.

We went back to the large hall where the Lion, the Scarecrow, and the Tin Woodman were waiting for us.

The Lion stopped pacing when he saw us. "What did the Wizard say?" he asked.

"It's impossible," Dorothy answered, drying her eyes. "The Wizard will not send me home until I have killed the Wicked Witch of the West...and that I can never do."

She plopped down in an emerald chair and described the Wizard's bizarre appearance. Hoping to offer some comfort, I sat in her lap.

"I hope you have better luck than I do," Dorothy said to her friends as she slowly stroked my fur.

Just then, the soldier arrived. "You're next!" he said, pointing to the Scarecrow. They walked together toward the Throne Room.

A few minutes later, the Scarecrow was back.

"The Wizard told me the same thing he told you," the Scarecrow said. "I would have to kill the

Wicked Witch of the West before he would give me any brains."

"But here's the oddest part," he added, "this time he wasn't a floating head. He was a giant snowflake!"

*That sounds crazy!* I thought. *Maybe the Scarecrow was fibbing. But everyone else seemed to believe him, so I decided to believe him, too.*

Both the Lion and the Tin Woodman told us they got the same demand from the Wizard when they saw him: "Kill the Wicked Witch of the West!"

When he met with the Lion, however, the Wizard took the form of a glowing ball of fire. And when he spoke to the Tin Woodman, he transformed himself into an elephant-sized beast with the head of a rhinoceros.

*Strange...very strange.*

"What shall we do now?" Dorothy asked.

"There is only one thing we can do," replied the Lion. "We must go to the Land of the Winkies and destroy the Wicked Witch of the West!"

"But what if we can't?" she asked.

"Then I'll never have courage," the Lion said.

"And I'll never have any brains," the Scarecrow said.

"And I'll never have a heart," the Tin Woodman added.

"And I," said Dorothy, "will never see my Auntie Em and Uncle Henry again."

*And I'll never play with Millie...or see my ball*, I thought.

"Then we must try!" Dorothy declared, quickly rising from the emerald chair.

"I'll go with you," the Lion said, "but I'm probably too much of a coward to kill the Wicked Witch."

"I'll go, too," the Scarecrow said, "but since I'm such a fool, I won't be any help at all."

*That's probably true*, I thought.

"And I don't have the heart to harm anyone... even a Witch," the Tin Woodman said. "But if you all go, count me in!"

"Then it's decided!" Dorothy said. "We'll leave first thing in the morning!"

We exchanged goodbyes and walked to our different rooms. After another tasty dinner, Dorothy and I went right to sleep.

The next morning, we woke to the crowing of a green rooster. Dorothy washed up and got dressed. Then we joined the rest of our group in the hall.

The green girl appeared and filled Dorothy's basket with lots of good things to eat. I showed my appreciation by licking her hand. She didn't seem to mind. As a matter of fact, she giggled.

As soon as the soldier arrived to lead us to the gate, the green girl bowed and walked away. Before she was completely out of sight, she turned around and called out, "Good luck!"

Yes, I thought. *We'll certainly need that!*

The soldier led us through the sparkling streets of the Emerald City until we reached the Keeper of the Gate. He collected our glasses and put them back in the shiny box.

"Which road will take us to the Wicked Witch of the West?" Dorothy asked the Gatekeeper.

"There aren't any roads," he replied.

"Why not?" asked the Lion.

"Because no one ever wants to go there."

*Hmm...that makes sense.*

"How can we find her, then?" the Scarecrow asked.

"That will be easy," the Gatekeeper answered. "Just go in the direction of the setting sun. When the Wicked Witch discovers you're looking for her, she'll come and get you."

*Uh-oh!* I thought. *That doesn't sound so good.* I was nervously pawing the ground.

Dorothy thanked the Gatekeeper for all his help and we were on our way...again.

We travelled over grassy hills filled with daisies and buttercups. *There were no poppies, thank goodness!* After a while, I turned to look at the fading light of the Emerald City. *We'll be back soon...I hope.*

All of a sudden, a blue-and-yellow butterfly flew past me. I couldn't help myself. I started chasing it over one of the hills.

"Toto, come back!" Dorothy called out. "We've got to stay together!"

I didn't mind Dorothy telling me what to do. But then the Scarecrow yelled, "Come back NOW, Toto! You're slowing us down!"

I CAN'T BELIEVE IT! I thought. THAT ALWAYS-

FALLING-DOWN SCARECROW ACTUALLY SAID I WAS SLOWING EVERYONE DOWN!?!

I raced back and loudly barked at him. He didn't seem to mind. He actually poked the Tin Woodman and they both chuckled. Now I was really fuming.

Then I had a mean thought. I wished for something bad to happen to the Scarecrow again so that he wouldn't be able to travel with us anymore. Yes, I know that was a horrible thing to wish for...but I was very, very angry.

Dorothy told me to calm down and stop barking. After a while, I did.

We climbed up and down a few small hills until we came to a flat meadow. With the sun shining directly on our faces, Dorothy, the Lion, and I were getting tired.

While the Tin Woodman and that annoying Scarecrow stood guard, the rest of us took naps.

It was probably only a few minutes later when the Tin Woodman shouted with alarm, "Wake up, everybody!" He pointed to the western sky. "Look!"

It was a terrifying sight! Hundreds of monkeys

with large wings were flying directly toward us!

"They must have been sent by the Wicked Witch!" Dorothy cried out. "She knows we're here!"

Before we could run away, some of the monkeys caught the Scarecrow and pulled out all his straw. Then they threw his clothing into the top branches of a tall tree.

*Oh, no!* I thought. *My wish about the Scarecrow has come true! What have I done?*

Other monkeys grabbed the Tin Woodman and carried him through the air. Then they dropped him on some sharp rocks. He was so battered and dented he couldn't move or make a sound.

*This is terrible!* I thought, trembling with fear. *What's going to happen now?*

I didn't have to wait long to find out. Two of them tied pieces of thick rope around the Lion's head and legs so that he couldn't bite or scratch. They lifted him into the air and flew into the sky.

*Where are they taking our poor friend?* I wondered.

Dorothy held me in her arms. "I won't let anyone hurt you," she whispered. "I promise."

The largest monkey landed in front of Dorothy. He was the only one wearing a hat – a red soldier's hat. *He must be their leader*, I thought.

It looked as if he was about to strike Dorothy, but he noticed her forehead and stopped. "I will not harm this young girl," he declared, "for she is protected by the Good Witch of the North!"

"What are you going to do with us?" Dorothy asked, squeezing me tighter.

"The Wicked Witch of the West has commanded that we bring you to her castle. And that is what we will do!"

In an instant, we were flying across the sky. I looked down and saw the Scarecrow's straw scattered over the ground. *If the Scarecrow ever gets put back together, I vowed, I'll never wish for anything bad to happen to him again. I'll even try to be his friend.*

We travelled over hills and valleys. I felt the cold wind rush against my face. After what seemed like a long time, I could see a large castle up ahead. The leader of the monkeys flew downward and brought us to the entrance.

"Here they are," the leader said to someone we could barely see, "as you wished."

Then all of them flew off, darkening the sky.

I wasn't sorry to see them go. *Goodbye scary monkeys...and don't ever come back!*

Stepping out of the shadows, someone was waiting for us. Dressed all in black, from her shoes to her pointy hat, it had to be her...the Wicked Witch of the West!

# Chapter 13

# The Wicked Witch of the West

"Welcome to my castle," the Wicked Witch said. "It's so nice of you to come."

Her words might have sounded friendly, but

Dorothy and I weren't fooled. "Where's the Lion?" she asked. "What have you done with him?"

I couldn't believe the terrible odor of that Witch...a combination of cooked cabbage and rotting apples. This was one of the times I wished my sense of smell wasn't so strong.

"Don't worry about your friend," the Wicked Witch replied. She had the meanest face I had ever seen. It was green, too. "He's locked up in the courtyard, but I have plans for him. Whenever I go into town, he'll pull my chariot."

Dorothy gasped.

"He's still better off than your other companions," the Witch cackled.

Of course she was referring to the Scarecrow and the Tin Woodman. *Will they ever be okay again?* I wondered.

"I want to see him now!" Dorothy demanded.

"You'll see the Lion when I say so!" the Wicked Witch snarled, moving so close that her bumpy nose was almost touching Dorothy's face. "Don't you understand, my dear. You, your dog, and the

Lion are my prisoners...forever!"

Dorothy began to sob. I felt like doing the same, except dogs can't cry. I whimpered instead.

The Wicked Witch stepped back and stared at Dorothy. She frowned when she saw the Good Witch's mark on Dorothy's forehead. Then she looked down at Dorothy's feet. Her green face turned red and her eyes flashed with rage.

"What are you doing with the Witch of the East's silver shoes?" she shrieked. "You must have killed her, you horrid creature!"

"It was an accident," Dorothy explained. "My house fell on top of her."

"I don't care!" the Wicked Witch yelled. "Hand them over. They belong to me now!"

Dorothy immediately stopped crying, stood up straight, and glared at the Wicked Witch. "No, I won't!" she declared. "If you want them so much, they must be very powerful!"

*Atta girl, Dorothy! Don't let that mean, ugly witch boss you around!*

"I'll get them later!" the Wicked Witch said,

quickly turning on her heels and marching toward the castle's entrance.

I saw men in yellow uniforms guarding the castle. *Those must be the Winkies!* I thought. The Winkies were staring straight ahead. It looked as if they were under the Wicked Witch's spell.

"Come with me!" the Wicked Witch commanded. "I've got lots of work for you to do!"

We followed the Wicked Witch through her gloomy castle. Her crooked form cast a frightening shadow on the wall. I was just about to bite one of her heels, when Dorothy saw me and silently shook her head no.

"What's going on back there?" the Wicked Witch called out.

*How did she see us? She must have eyes in the back of her head.*

"Nothing," Dorothy answered quickly.

Only a few rays of sunlight peeked through the narrow windows. Dorothy whispered the names beneath the portraits of mean-looking witches that hung on the brick walls: "Horribeth," "Agratz," and "Nastina."

Dorothy's silver shoes clattered on the cement floor as we walked along quickly. "I wonder where the Wicked Witch is taking us," she said to me in a low voice.

Before I could respond with a puzzled yip, the Wicked Witch turned around and yelled, "Hush! You'll find out soon enough where you're going!"

*I wish we had another house to fall on you,* I thought.

Finally we arrived at a large kitchen.

"Now get to work!" the Witch said, pointing to a broom. "When I return, I expect this floor to be spotless!" She stormed out.

"I guess I'd better do what she wants...for now," Dorothy said, taking the broom in her hands.

Bits of dried-up food were scattered across the floor. *What a mess!* Dorothy slowly swept everything into a dustpan. When it was full, she emptied it into a battered garbage can.

"The floor is still dirty," Dorothy said, looking down, "and that Wicked Witch wants it spotless."

Dorothy searched inside the pantry until she found a bucket and a mop.

"This mop is stiff," she said, brushing off its cobwebs. "It hasn't been used in years. That's why the floor is so filthy."

Dorothy took the bucket to the Witch's sink. "The faucet's rusted shut!" she exclaimed. At long last, after trying and trying, she was able to turn on the water. She filled up the bucket and started mopping. Not able to help, I just sat and watched.

A few minutes later, the Wicked Witch appeared with a small box in her hands. She stared at Dorothy. "What are you doing with that bucket of water?" she screeched.

"I'm cleaning the floor," Dorothy replied, "just like you asked me to."

"I never asked you to wash it!" the Witch cried out. "Now move that bucket away from me!"

Using her foot, Dorothy slid the bucket to a corner of the kitchen. When a few drops of water splashed near the Witch, she shivered with fear and took a quick step back.

*That's odd,* I thought. *Why is she so scared? It's just a little water.*

All of a sudden, the Witch's expression changed. Smiling, she displayed her yellowish teeth as she opened the small box. It contained a pair of pink fluffy slippers.

"Your feet must be sore, my dear," she said in her "pretend" sweet voice. "Why don't you take off those uncomfortable shoes and try these on instead?"

"Absolutely not!" Dorothy exclaimed. "I know what you really want!"

"Horned toads and spiders!" the Wicked Witch shrieked. "You miserable creature! I'll get those silver shoes! Just you wait and see!"

I heard the Wicked Witch mutter some magical words as she pointed to a space in front of Dorothy. She must have created something invisible, because Dorothy tripped and fell. One of her silver shoes flew off.

*Oh, no!* I thought. *What's going to happen now?*

The Wicked Witch quickly grabbed the shoe and put it on.

Dorothy jumped up and yelled, "Give me back my shoe!" She was angrier than I'd ever seen her.

"Never!" the Wicked Witch replied. "And soon I'll have the other one, too!"

I really wanted to help Dorothy, but what could I do? Then I remembered! The Witch had seemed frightened of water. But why? It didn't matter! I raced over to the bucket and barked...and barked... and barked.

Thank goodness Dorothy got my message. Quick as a wink, she picked up the bucket and threw the water all over the Wicked Witch.

You just won't believe what happened next! It was the strangest thing I'd ever seen...really! The Witch actually began to melt.

"Look what you've done, you horrible creature!" she screamed, sinking into the floor. "I never thought a little girl like you could defeat a powerful witch like me!" With those last words, she became a shapeless puddle on the floor.

Speechless, we couldn't stop staring.

"The Wicked Witch is gone...FOREVER!" Dorothy

said, reaching down to give me a tender squeeze. "How did you know that water would melt her? You're amazing!" I couldn't explain, so I just looked up at her smiling face and wagged my tail.

Dorothy picked up the silver shoe, dried it with a cloth, and put it back on her foot.

"Now let's find the Lion!" she said, charging out the door.

# Chapter 14

# The Lion Is Free!

In my excitement, I raced ahead of Dorothy.
I scampered down the hallway, hoping to pick up the
Lion's scent. The nails on my paws made a clickety-

clackety sound on the cement floor.

"Wait for me!" Dorothy called out. I skidded to a halt to let her catch up. "All right, Toto," she said, catching her breath, "you lead the way."

No *problem*, I thought, proudly wagging my tail as I trotted along. With Dorothy close behind, I turned a few corners and found the courtyard. The Lion was lying on the hard ground, fast asleep.

I loudly barked, rousing the Lion from his slumber. When he saw us, he lifted his head and roared with happiness. "It's you!" he exclaimed, bounding over to us. "I thought I'd never see you again!"

Dorothy found the key on a hook and unlocked the gate. The Lion jumped up and put his front paws on Dorothy's shoulders, almost knocking her over.

*Whoa, big fella!* I thought. *Don't hurt her.*

"Where's the Wicked Witch?" the Lion asked. "Is she coming after you?"

Dorothy shook her head and explained how we melted the Wicked Witch with a bucket of water. "She'll never bother us again."

"Great job, you two!" the Lion declared. "Now let's get out of here!"

"Yes," Dorothy said, "but first I must tell the Winkies what happened. They were only guarding the castle for the Wicked Witch because they were under her spell."

After we walked outside, Dorothy called for the Winkies to join us. They slowly gathered, anxiously looking around for the Wicked Witch. It was obvious they didn't know what had just happened to her.

"The Wicked Witch of the West has been destroyed," Dorothy announced. "You are free... now and forever!"

The Winkies cheered and threw their yellow hats in the air. It was the beginning of the wildest celebration I had ever seen. They sang joyful songs and danced all over the place.

*Just don't step on me*, I thought as I jumped away from their fast-moving feet.

"If only the Scarecrow and the Tin Woodman were here with us," the Lion said to Dorothy, "then I'd really be happy."

Dorothy silenced the Winkies by raising her arms. "We need some help," she said. "Two of our friends are missing. One is a Tin Woodman and the other is a Scarecrow. They were badly injured by the flying monkeys. Will you help us find them?"

"Of course!" one of the Winkies called out. "You have freed us from the Wicked Witch of the West. We'll do anything you ask!"

"So, what are we waiting for?" Dorothy said. "Let's go!"

A group of Winkies led us to a rocky meadow. We found the Tin Woodman lying motionless on the ground, all battered and bent. The handle of his trusty axe was broken off.

"Goodness me!" Dorothy exclaimed. "He's worse off than I thought."

"It's getting dark," one of the Winkies said. "Let's take care of this poor fellow first." He tenderly picked up the Tin Woodman. "We'll return first thing tomorrow morning for your other friend."

*Really?* I thought. *Shouldn't we be bringing back the Scarecrow, too?* But Dorothy agreed, so

I agreed, too.

When we arrived back at the castle, Dorothy asked, "Are there any tinsmiths here?"

I wasn't sure what a tinsmith was, but I knew it must have something to do with the Tin Woodman.

"Oh, yes!" one of the Winkies said.

Three tinsmiths were called in and immediately got to work. They hammered away, and screwed some metal plates onto his chest, his back, and both of his legs. When they were done, the Tin Woodman was as good as new.

"Thank you so much for saving me!" he exclaimed, slowly bending his arms and legs.

Dorothy told the Tin Woodman all that had happened after the flying monkeys had dropped him on the rocks.

"Unbelievable!" he exclaimed. Turning to me, he continued, "Toto, you're a true hero!"

*Me, a hero? Can that really be? All I did was bark at a bucket of water. Dorothy's the real hero. She threw the water on the Witch. Well...I did help her know what to do. Hey, maybe I am a hero. 'Toto the hero!*' I liked the way that sounded.

"And don't worry about the Scarecrow," Dorothy said. "We'll find him tomorrow and fix him up, too!" Remembering that the Scarecrow and I were now friends, I yipped and wagged my tail.

Early the next morning, some of the Winkies joined us in search of the Scarecrow.

"There he is!" Dorothy called out when we came to a tall tree. I looked up and saw the Scarecrow's clothes on some of the higher branches. But his straw was gone, blown away by the wind. It was a very sad sight.

"We can't climb up there," the Lion said. "What are we going to do? "

"Don't worry," the Tin Woodman said as he began to chop down the tree. After a few swings with his sharp axe, I saw the tree falling. *Uh-oh!* It was coming toward me. I quickly darted out of the way. *Whew...just in time.*

When the tree hit the ground, the Scarecrow's clothes were scattered everywhere. I picked up the Scarecrow's hat with my teeth, and Dorothy gathered the rest of his clothing.

Back at the castle, the Winkies stuffed clear, crisp straw into the Scarecrow's shirt. As soon as they were done, the Scarecrow began to move around. He happily thanked everyone... including me!

I positioned my head under the Scarecrow's hand, encouraging him to pet me. It felt scratchy, but good.

For the third time, Dorothy told the story about how she and I had melted the Wicked Witch...this time to the Scarecrow. I didn't care. *I'll never get tired of hearing it*, I thought.

"That's fantastic!" the Scarecrow said, "but what do we do now?"

"We must return to the Emerald City at once," Dorothy replied. "Now that we've done what the Wizard asked, he'll *have* to grant our wishes!"

Our merry band spent one last night in the castle. Early the next morning, Dorothy filled her basket with snacks and drinks. A large crowd of Winkies was waiting to say goodbye when we walked outside the front door.

For some reason, the Winkies seemed to especially like the Tin Woodman. "Please stay here and be our ruler," a few of them called out. *Maybe it's because he's so shiny*, I wondered.

But the Tin Woodman was determined to get a heart from the Wizard, and politely declined their offer.

Just then, one of the Winkies stepped forward with a golden box. "Before you go," she said to Dorothy, "we want to show our appreciation with some gifts."

*Oh boy!* I thought. *I hope there's something in there for me.*

I wasn't disappointed. The first gift was a golden collar...just the right size for a Cairn terrier. She handed it to Dorothy, who fastened it around my neck. (There was a bigger collar for the Lion, too.)

The Winkie presented the Scarecrow with a gold walking stick. *That's a swell idea!* I thought. *Now he won't fall down so much.* The next gift was a silver oilcan for the Tin Woodman.

*What about Dorothy?* I wondered. *After all,*

*she got rid of the Wicked Witch for you...with my assistance, of course!*

I didn't need to worry. "And this is for Dorothy," the Winkie said, handing her a golden cap that was covered with diamonds and rubies.

"It's beautiful!" Dorothy said.

"Yes!" the Winkie agreed. "And it has a special power, too!"

"How exciting!" Dorothy exclaimed. "What kind of power?"

"When you wear the Golden Cap and say the magic words, the flying monkeys will come and grant you a wish. You may summon them three times. The magic words are on the cap's lining. Isn't that wonderful?"

*Are you kidding me?* I thought. *I never want to see those awful monkeys ever again!* I looked at my friends to see their reactions. They all seemed horrified...including Dorothy.

"But the monkeys brought us to the Wicked Witch," Dorothy said, putting the Golden Cap inside her basket. "Aren't they our enemies?"

"The Wicked Witch was wearing the Golden Cap when she commanded them," the Winkie said. "They were powerless to disobey her."

I was starting to get impatient with all this standing around. *Time's a wastin'!* That's what Uncle Henry would say if he were here.

After lots of hugging and many good wishes, we finally left the Land of the Winkies.

"Since there are no roads to guide us, we must travel toward the rising sun!" the Scarecrow declared, pointing east. "That's the way to the Emerald City."

*What a smart guy!* I thought.

All through the morning, we walked past large fields of flowers. At one point, while everyone was trudging along, I decided to run ahead. Bad idea! When I stopped and turned around, there was no one in sight.

I barked. I yelped. I whimpered. *Where is everyone?*

Suddenly, I heard someone calling my name. But it wasn't Dorothy who found me...it was the Scarecrow. What a nice surprise! I almost licked his hand, but decided against it. I didn't want any pieces of straw on my tongue.

When he brought me back to my friends, Dorothy told me not to run ahead ever again. *You don't have to worry about that!* I thought, my tail between my legs.

"Now that it's noon, and the sun is directly above us," the Scarecrow said, "I can't tell which way is east anymore."

"Let's just keep walking," Dorothy said, "we'll have to arrive somewhere soon."

But after continuing for another hour or so, there were still no houses...and certainly no sign of the Emerald City! "We're lost," Dorothy said as she sat down on the grass.

A striped butterfly flew past my head. For the first time in my life, I was too hot and tired to chase after it. I just lay there and panted.

"I have an idea!" the Tin Woodman called out. "If Dorothy says the magic words inside the Golden Cap, we can ask the flying monkeys to fly us to the Emerald City!"

WHAT!?! I thought, perking up my ears. *The hot*

*sun must be getting to you!*

"Don't you remember what they did to us?" the Scarecrow asked.

"Of course I remember," the Tin Woodman replied. "But we're lost...and we're running out of food and water."

Everyone, including me, turned to Dorothy. After all, she was our leader. "We have no choice," she said, taking out the Golden Cap. "Let's hope for the best."

She silently read the instructions on the inside lining of the cap and put it on her head. Standing on her left foot, she chanted, "Ep-pe, pep-pe."

Then she stood on her right foot. "Hil-lo, hol-lo." Back on both feet, she finished with these strange words: "Ziz-zy, zuz-zy, zik!"

In an instant, we heard the thunderous sound of flapping wings.

"Run for your lives!" the Scarecrow exclaimed as hundreds of flying monkeys flew toward us.

"Stay right here!" Dorothy cried out. "They're our only hope."

"If they attack us," the Lion declared, baring his

claws, "I'm ready to fight!"

But they didn't attack or threaten us in any way. Instead, the leader of the monkeys bowed before Dorothy, and asked, "What is your command?"

"We have lost our way," Dorothy replied, "and wish to go to the Emerald City. Can you help us?"

"We will take you right away," the leader declared. As soon as he said those words, two of the monkeys picked Dorothy up in their arms and flew away with her.

*Yikes!* I thought. *Bring her back!*

A moment later, six more monkeys lifted up the Scarecrow, the Tin Woodman, and the Lion – two monkeys each. Then a small monkey grabbed me and took off. Just like that, we were all up in the air, streaking across the sky.

*I hope this little guy doesn't drop me,* I thought. *I'm not that light!* After a while, I began to relax. I enjoyed watching the pretty gardens and tall trees whiz by.

I looked into the distance. There it was again, getting closer and closer...the Emerald City!

The flying monkeys gently dropped us off at the green gate. I gave a friendly yip to the monkey who was carrying me. *Nice job!* I thought. *Thanks for getting me here in one piece.*

As quickly as they had arrived, the flying monkeys were up in the sky and gone. I had mixed feelings about them. At first, we hated them. Then they saved our lives and brought us here. *Very confusing!*

Dorothy rang the bell and the Gatekeeper arrived. "Goodness gracious!" he said with surprise. "I thought you went to the castle of the Wicked Witch."

"We did!" the Tin Woodman exclaimed.

"How did you get away?"

"Dorothy melted her," the Scarecrow said. "And Toto helped, too."

"Excellent!" the Gatekeeper exclaimed. Then he crouched down by my side and said, "How are you, my brave friend?"

I could tell he wanted to pet me. Since he seemed friendly, I stretched out on the ground and let him scratch my belly. *Mmmm.*

All at once, the Gatekeeper stood up. Playtime

was over. He gave us our green glasses and led us back inside.

It was just as I had remembered...green... green...GREEN!

The Gatekeeper excitedly told some people that Dorothy and I had melted the Wicked Witch. Soon, a large crowd began following us to the Wizard's palace. They pointed to Dorothy and me, and shouted, "Hooray for Dorothy!" "Hooray for Toto!" "Dorothy's the greatest!" "We love you, Toto!"

I could tell Dorothy was embarrassed by all the attention she was getting, but I enjoyed it. *Would they have a parade for us? After all, we had now killed two evil witches. That's pretty good for a girl from Kansas and her clever dog.*

As I strutted along, I saw my reflection in one of the Tin Woodman's legs. *I look pretty spiffy with my new golden collar*, I thought.

We arrived at the palace, and the same soldier from our last visit let us in.

The green girl clapped her hands when she saw us. "Welcome back!" she called out cheerfully.

I think she was relieved we got out of the Wicked Witch's castle alive.

"When will the Wizard see us?" Dorothy said while the green girl guided us to our old rooms.

"I'm not sure," she replied. "But when he's ready, I'll let you know."

"Soon we'll be back in Kansas," Dorothy said to me. "I just know it!"

But the next day came and went without any word from the Wizard. And the day after that was the same.

There was plenty of good food to eat, so I had no complaints. I even noticed that my tummy was getting a little bigger. *When Millie sees me,* I thought, *she'll be surprised.*

"How can he treat us this way?" Dorothy said to our fellow travellers when we met in the palace's large hall the next day. "We did just what he asked us to do!"

The following morning, when the green girl arrived with our breakfast, there was still no message from the Wizard. "If he doesn't call for us at once," Dorothy warned, "tell him I'll summon the flying monkeys!"

The green girl left and came back in an instant. "He'll see you all at noon today," she announced with a smile. "I'll let the others know, too."

I yipped and barked and bounced up and down. *Hey, Wizard, don't mess with Dorothy!* I thought.

"We're going home!" Dorothy cried out.

Exactly at noon, the green girl brought our group to the Wizard's Throne Room and opened the door. *What would the Wizard look like this time?* I wondered.

We stared at the throne, but there was no Wizard in sight!

No floating head!

No giant snowflake!

No ball of fire!

No elephant-sized beast with the head of a rhino!

Nothing at all!!!

# Chapter 15

# Who Is that Man?

What's *going on here?* I thought. *Where is that
mysterious Wizard?*

I noticed a standing screen made out of wood
in the corner of the room. *Interesting,* I thought,
moving toward it. But before I got too close, I heard

Dorothy's voice.

"Toto, come back here!" she yelled. "Now!"

I scooted back to Dorothy's side. Everyone was nervously huddled together...waiting for something to happen.

At last, we heard a deep voice coming from the top of the domed ceiling.

"I am the great and terrible Wizard of Oz!" the voice boomed. "Why do you seek me?"

Well, let me tell you. Everyone was terrified. In fact, the Tin Woodman banged his knees together, which made a loud clank.

"Where are you?" Dorothy called out, looking around. "I can't see you."

"I am everywhere! But to mortals like you, I am invisible."

The Scarecrow was shaking so much that his hat fell off. I decided to do him a favor by picking it up with my teeth.

"Thank you, Toto," he whispered.

"I will now sit upon my throne," the Wizard's voice said. "You may talk to me there."

"We're here to have our wishes granted," Dorothy declared, facing the empty, bejeweled chair.

"What wishes?" the Wizard's voice asked.

*For a powerful Wizard, he's very forgetful,* I thought. *We were here only a week ago.*

"You promised to send Toto and me back to Kansas if we destroyed the Wicked Witch of the West...and we have!" After Dorothy spoke, the Scarecrow, the Lion, and the Tin Woodman reminded the Wizard about his promises to them, too.

"Is the Wicked Witch really destroyed?"

"Yes...of course!" Dorothy replied. "I melted her with a bucket of water."

"Well, this is quite a surprise!" the Wizard's voice said. "Frankly, I didn't expect to see you again. Come back tomorrow. I must have some time to think it over."

I looked at Dorothy. Her fists were clenched and her face was bright crimson.

"We've already waited a long time!" she exclaimed.

"And we're not going to wait any longer!" the Scarecrow added.

Unexpectedly, the Lion let out an ear-splitting roar.

*Bouncing biscuits!* He might have been only trying to scare the Wizard, but that angry Lion really startled me. I ran right into the screen. *Uh-oh!* It began to wobble back-and-forth, back-and-forth. *Please don't fall down*, I thought. But it did... CRASH! *Oops.*

A little old man was timidly standing there. He was almost as shocked as we were.

*Who are you?* I wanted to say. *Where's the Wizard?*

The Tin Woodman took over. "What are you doing here?" he yelled, rushing toward him.

"I'm...er...uh...the great and terrible...Wizard of Oz," the man said in a trembling voice.

"You can't be the Wizard of Oz!" Dorothy cried out. "The Wizard is a floating head. At least that's what he was when I saw him."

"I'm sorry," the man said. "The Wizard is not a floating head or a giant snowflake or a terrible beast or a ball of fire. All of that was make believe. It was just me...uh...pretending."

Everyone was stunned...especially Dorothy.

"So," she slowly said in a voice filled with disappointment, "does that mean there isn't any great and powerful Wizard of Oz?"

"I'm afraid not," the man said, looking down.

"You're a very bad man!" Dorothy shouted. I could see her eyes well up with tears. I felt like biting the phony Wizard.

"Oh, no, my dear," the man said. "I'm really a very good man, but I happen to be a very bad Wizard."

"You're a fraud!" the Scarecrow declared. "A great, big fake!"

"You're right about that," the Wizard agreed.

"But how did you appear in so many different forms?" Dorothy asked.

"It was all trickery," the man who called himself the Wizard said. "Let me show you." He led us to a small chamber in the rear of the Throne Room. (To keep things simple, I'll just call him the Wizard.)

The Wizard displayed the "floating head" (layers of paper with a painted face), the "giant snowflake" (a white cardboard cut-out), the "terrible beast" (lots of fabric sewn together with a papier-mâché animal head), and the "ball of fire" (a burning sphere of cotton covered with oil). He also showed us the thin, barely visible wire that suspended everything in the air.

"What about your voice?" Dorothy asked. "It seemed to be coming from different parts of the room."

"I am a ventriloquist," the Wizard said proudly. "That means I can throw the sound of my voice to wherever I wish."

I didn't understand what it meant to "throw" a voice, but the others in our group were nodding as if they knew what he was talking about. The only thing I like being thrown is my red ball with yellow dots.

"But none of this helps Toto and me get back to Kansas," Dorothy said.

"And that means no brains for me," the Scarecrow said.

"And no heart for me," the Tin Woodman said.

"And I'll be a coward for the rest of my life," the Lion added.

The Wizard closed his eyes as if deep in thought. Finally, he spoke. "I might not be a great Wizard," he said, "but perhaps I can help you get what you want. Please come back tomorrow morning and...Scarecrow, you shall have your brains; Tin Woodman, you shall have your heart; and Lion, you shall have your courage."

"Why should we believe you?" the Tin Woodman asked angrily.

I *agree*! I thought. *He tricked us before. He'll trick us again!*

"I can't give you any reason to trust me," the Wizard said with a sincere expression, "but this time I really mean it."

He must have convinced them because the Lion, the Tin Woodman, and the Scarecrow were all beaming with delight.

After a few moments, however, the Scarecrow glanced at Dorothy and realized she was crying. "Wait a minute!" he exclaimed. "What about Dorothy and Toto? You didn't mention them!"

"Yes," Dorothy said, wiping away a tear. "What about us?"

"Hmm," the Wizard said, rubbing his chin with

his thumb and forefinger, "I think I'll be able to help you, too."

"Really?" Dorothy exclaimed. "That would be wonderful!"

*Poor kid,* I thought. *You shouldn't believe everything this fraud says.* But I could tell by her expression that she had gotten her hopes up again. I couldn't blame her.

We were leaving the Throne Room when the Wizard suddenly called after us. "Have I told you how I arrived at the Emerald City and became the Wizard of Oz?"

Dorothy shook her head.

"Shall I tell you?" he asked. "I've never told anyone. But it might take quite a bit of time."

*NO! Please, no!* I thought. *Haven't we been through enough already? Please...PLEASE...say no. Can't we just go upstairs?*

"Yes, I'd like to hear it," Dorothy said as she turned around and walked back. The rest of us followed her. I don't think she noticed me lagging behind with my annoyed expression.

Well, as you can imagine, it was the most boring "blah, blah, blah" story that's ever been told. I've forgotten much of what he said, but here's what I do remember:

### The Wizard's Story (as remembered by Toto)

The Wizard of Oz originally grew up in Omaha, Nebraska. ("That's not that far from Kansas!" Dorothy exclaimed.) When he was a young man, he became a balloonist for a travelling circus. On "Circus Day," his job was to go up in a hot-air balloon to attract ticket buyers.

One day, his balloon ropes got twisted and he drifted above the clouds. A current of air carried him many miles away. After a day and a night of windswept travel, he landed in a strange and beautiful country...Oz. ("Just like Toto and me!" Dorothy announced.) When the people who lived here saw him come down from the clouds, they thought he was a great Wizard. And he let them believe it. (*Not too surprising!*)

They were afraid of him and promised to do

anything he wanted. So, he ordered them to build a city — the Emerald City! — and a huge palace, too. (*Pretty selfish, huh?*) To make it a true "Emerald City" where everything was green, the big faker ordered people to wear green glasses. (*Unbelievable! This guy is really something!*)

When Dorothy heard that part about the glasses, she interrupted him. "Does that mean the Emerald City isn't really green?" she asked.

"No more than any other city," he replied.

"Will we be blinded if we take off our green glasses?" the Scarecrow asked.

"No, not at all," the Wizard replied with a smile, "but please keep them on, my friends. Everyone here thinks I'm a great Wizard. I don't want to spoil their illusions."

Not caring what people thought, I rapidly shook my head from side to side, hoping to throw off my glasses. But they were locked on tight. Dorothy, much to my disappointment, agreed with his ridiculous request. So we kept our glasses on.

Anyway, back to the Wizard's story:

He has lived in this palace for many years. In order to keep his true identity a secret, he hasn't let anyone see what he really looks like, except us! And...now that both evil witches are dead (thanks to Dorothy and me), there's nothing for him to be afraid of. (*But if he doesn't grant Dorothy's wish, he'll really have something to fear...me!*)

His story was finally over. *Whew!*

I led everyone to the door. *Let's go before he tells any more stories*, I thought.

"I'll do my best to make your wishes come true!" the Wizard called out while we were leaving. "See you tomorrow!"

"I know he's not a true Wizard," Dorothy said as we entered our room, "but he seems like a nice fellow. Maybe he can still help us get back home."

*I hope so*, I thought, *but I really can't say I believed him.*

# Chapter 16

# The Wizard's Magic

Early the next morning, with the Scarecrow leading the way, we marched to the Throne Room and knocked on the door.

"Please enter," the Wizard said in a gentle voice, waving us inside.

"I have come for my brains!" the Scarecrow declared.

"Oh, yes," the Wizard said. He pointed to a high-backed chair and asked the Scarecrow to sit down.

"Please excuse me, but I must take your head off," the Wizard said. "I need to put your new brains in their proper place."

No, Scarecrow, NO! I thought. Don't let him near you! He's a faker! Somebody stop him!

I barked my head off...oops, sorry. I mean I barked like mad, but nobody stopped anything. In fact, Dorothy was angry with me. "Enough, Toto!" she said. "Calm down."

"You may take my head off," the Scarecrow said with a chuckle, "as long as you make it better before you put it back on."

Well, let me tell you...it was a very unusual sight! The Wizard lifted up the Scarecrow's head, placed it on a table, and took out all the straw. Then he poured bran from a cereal box into the Scarecrow's empty head until it was full.

I couldn't quite believe what I was seeing. *That's*

*the stuff people eat for breakfast,* I thought. *What in the world is he doing?*

The Wizard put the Scarecrow's bursting-with-bran head back on his body. "Now you will be a great man," he said, "for I have given you a lot of 'bran-new' brains."

*Are you kidding me?* I thought. *That's the worst joke I ever heard!*

But the Wizard wasn't laughing and the Scarecrow, that trusting fellow, seemed to be satisfied.

"Thank you!" he said to the Wizard.

"How do you feel?" Dorothy lovingly asked the Scarecrow.

"I feel very wise," he replied. "And when I get used to my new brains, I shall know everything."

*Well, if he feels okay about having "bran brains,"* I thought, *maybe it's OK. Who can really know what's better for a scarecrow, anyway – a head stuffed with straw or a head stuffed with bran?*

"My turn!" the Tin Woodman called out. "I am ready for my heart."

"Very well," answered the Wizard. "But I'll have

to remove this metal plate from your chest so I can put your heart in the right place." He picked up a screwdriver. "I hope this won't hurt you."

"Don't worry," answered the Tin Woodman. "I won't feel a thing."

After taking out the metal plate, the Wizard opened a dresser drawer and took out something red and shiny.

"It's a heart made of silk and sawdust," the Wizard announced. "Isn't it a beauty?"

"Yes," replied the Tin Woodman, "but is it a kind heart?"

*Oh, that Tin Woodman,* I thought. *Such a sweet guy.*

"Of course!" replied the Wizard as he placed the silk heart inside the Tin Woodman's chest and screwed the metal plate back on. "Now you have a heart that would make anyone feel proud."

The Tin Woodman beamed as he bowed. "I am very grateful to you," he said, "and I shall never forget your kindness."

A silk-and-sawdust heart seemed pretty silly to me, but the Tin Woodman was happy with it.

*And that's what matters,* I thought.

Just then, the Lion spoke up. "Can I have my courage now?" he asked gruffly.

"Yes, indeed," replied the Wizard, "I will get it for you."

*What's he going to do now?* I wondered.

The Wizard went to a cupboard and took down a green bottle from a high shelf. He poured a thick green liquid into a green dish. I jumped up on one of the chairs to get a better view.

*That certainly doesn't look like courage to me,* I thought.

"Drink, please," the Wizard said, offering the dish to the Lion.

"What is it?" the Lion asked, sniffing the green liquid and making a sour face.

"Well," replied the Wizard, "if it were inside you, it would be courage. You know, of course, that courage is always inside; so this can't be called courage until you've swallowed it."

*What a bunch of mumbo-jumbo!* I thought. *My King-of-the-Jungle friend can't possibly believe this nonsense! He's too smart...right?*

But the Lion slurped down every drop.

"How do you feel now?" the Wizard asked.

"Full of courage!" the Lion exclaimed as he bounded back to us.

*My goodness!* I thought. *I give up!*

While the Lion, the Scarecrow, and the Tin Woodman congratulated one another, Dorothy stood in one spot...waiting silently.

*Hey, Wizard!* I thought. *There's nothing in your cupboard or chest of drawers to get Dorothy and me back to Kansas, is there? You're going to disappoint us again. I know it!*

The Wizard slowly turned and fixed his gaze on Dorothy.

"Let's go outside!" he announced. "It's time to go home!"

# Chapter 17

# The Hot Air Balloon Takes Off!

"Really?" Dorothy said. "Right now?"

*That Wizard had better be telling us the truth, I thought, or else he's in deep trouble!*

"Follow me," the Wizard said, stopping for a moment to put on his green top hat.

"What's going on?" the Scarecrow asked.

"Now that I have my new brains, I need to know everything."

"After I told you my story yesterday," the Wizard explained as we walked along, "I realized how much I missed Omaha, my hometown. And now that both of the evil Witches are gone, the people of Oz are safe. It's the perfect time for me to leave."

"That makes perfect sense!" the Scarecrow said, nodding his head.

"But how would I get there?" the Wizard continued. "Then I remembered that my old hot-air balloon is still here...in the palace cellar. With some repairs, it would be perfect for taking me to Omaha and Dorothy to Kansas."

*Don't forget about me, bub!* I thought. *I'm going back to Kansas, too, you know.*

"Where is your hot-air balloon now?" the Tin Woodman asked.

"In front of the palace," the Wizard replied. "My helpers worked on it all night long. It's fixed up and ready to go!"

We arrived at the palace door. With a grand

flourish, he opened it.

What a sight! There must have been a thousand people from the Emerald City surrounding a gigantic hot-air balloon. The balloon part was bright green (not a surprise) and it was connected to a big basket.

*Uh-oh!* I thought. *Is that thing going to take Dorothy and me all the way to Kansas? This could be as scary as Dorothy's flying house.*

The green balloon was rapidly filling up with hot air from fiery burners directly underneath it. The strong ropes that connected the basket to heavy sandbags on the ground kept it from flying away.

"It's so beautiful!" Dorothy exclaimed.

*I just hope it's safe,* I thought.

When the people saw the Wizard, they started to call out, "All hail the powerful Wizard of Oz!" and "The Wizard is great!" Stuff like that.

*Are they serious?* I thought. *This little old man doesn't look like a powerful Wizard to me. But no one seemed to be bothered by his appearance.*

"Why are you leaving us?" someone called out.

"I'm...er...uh...going to visit my great brother

Wizard who lives in the clouds," he replied.

*Good grief! This guy can't stop fibbing, can he?*

"While I'm gone," the Wizard continued, "the Scarecrow will rule over you. He'll be a kind and wise leader. Please obey him as you would me."

I guess the Scarecrow liked that idea. He smiled and waved to the cheering crowd.

We followed the Wizard down the steps. As the balloon expanded with hot air, it tugged harder and harder on the ropes.

"Hurry up, Dorothy!" the Wizard cried out, stepping into the hot-air balloon. "It's ready to take off!" *He forgot about me again*, I thought. *Whatever!*

"This is happening so fast!" Dorothy said as she quickly hugged the Scarecrow, the Tin Woodman, and the Lion.

"Goodbye," she said, tearfully. "I'm going to miss you."

Dorothy was just about to scoop me up and step inside when I saw Catherine in the crowd... and she was holding Missy Boots. *What a surprise!*

I don't know what got into me, but I took off. I just had to say goodbye to Missy Boots. As soon as

I reached her, I heard Dorothy's loud voice. "Toto! Toto!"

When I turned around and saw the anxious expression on her face, I realized what a terrible mistake I had made. *Foolish Toto!*

"Dorothy!" the Wizard shouted. "The balloon is taking off! Get in!"

"I won't leave without Toto," I heard her say. *That's my girl!*

I rushed back to Dorothy, who quickly lifted me up. Holding me, she ran toward the balloon...closer and closer. But as soon as we arrived...CRACK! The ropes broke and the balloon instantly rose into the air...without us. No! No! NO!!!

"Come back!" Dorothy called out.

"I'm sorry, but I can't make it go down!" the Wizard shouted as the balloon took off into the sky. He waved his top hat and yelled, "Goodbye, everyone!"

Sadly, I watched the Wizard's balloon getting smaller and smaller and smaller. Soon it became a tiny dot...and then it was gone.

*It's entirely my fault!* I thought. *I've ruined*

*everything!*

I sat down and started whimpering. The Scarecrow must have felt sorry for me because he bent over and stroked my fur for a little while. That was nice, but I was still miserable.

*Dorothy must be so angry with me,* I thought. *Will she ever forgive me?*

A few minutes later, Dorothy knelt by my side and began to pet me. She was crying. I realized then that she wasn't mad...just disappointed and sad.

"That was our last hope of getting home, Toto," she said, "our very last hope."

# Chapter 18

# The Flying Monkeys Return

The Scarecrow, the Tin Woodman, and the Lion gathered around Dorothy and me.

"Please don't be upset," the Lion said in his most comforting growl.

"With all my heart," the Tin Woodman added, "I was hoping you'd stay here with us."

Then it was the Scarecrow's turn. "You could help me rule the Emerald City," he said in his wisest voice.

"You're all such good friends," Dorothy said, wiping away a tear, "but I must find a way to go home to Auntie Em and Uncle Henry."

Dorothy's words made me think about Millie again. *Is she chasing squirrels without me?* I wondered. *Does she even still remember me?*

"What do we do now?" the Tin Woodman asked.

"Let me think," the Scarecrow said, lightly tapping his forehead.

We all looked at him...and waited.

"Let's call the flying monkeys again," he declared, "and ask them to carry you and Toto to Kansas."

*Really?* I thought. *Is that your best plan? There must be something else we can do.*

"That's a wonderful idea!" Dorothy exclaimed. She immediately ran to our room and came back with the Golden Cap. She put it on, spoke the magic words, and the band of flying monkeys quickly returned.

"This is the second time you have called us," the leader said, bowing before Dorothy. "What is your wish?"

"I want you to fly Toto and me to a faraway

land called Kansas."

"We can help you in many ways," the monkey leader said, "but we cannot leave Oz. I'm sorry." He spread his wings and flew away, his buddies trailing close behind.

"Oh, my," Dorothy said. "Not only am I still here, I have wasted another of the Golden Cap's three wishes!"

The Scarecrow's face brightened. "I'll ask the soldier who brought us to the Wizard," he said. "Maybe he'll have some good advice."

The soldier was summoned and stood at attention before his new leader, the Scarecrow.

"Dorothy wishes to leave Oz and go home to Kansas," the Scarecrow said with authority. "How can she get there?"

"I'm not sure," the soldier said, "but Glinda might be able to help."

"Who's that?" the Lion asked.

"Glinda is a good and powerful Witch. She lives in a large castle in the Land of the South."

"Oh, yes!" Dorothy said. "I remember hearing about her from the Witch of the North. How do we get there?"

"Take that road by the stream," the soldier replied, pointing with his sword. "But there is a dangerous forest on the way."

*Fiddlesticks! I thought. Another obstacle! I guess I shouldn't complain. It's because of me we're in this mess.*

The soldier saluted and marched off.

"In spite of the trouble that lies ahead," the Scarecrow said, "I think the best thing for Dorothy is to journey to the Land of the South and ask for Glinda's help."

"You are wise indeed, Scarecrow," Dorothy said.

"I'll go with Dorothy, too!" the Lion announced. "She will need someone to protect her."

"And I shall also accompany Dorothy," the Tin Woodman said. "My trusty axe may be of service to her."

"Well, then," the Scarecrow said, "let's get ready."

"Are you coming, too?" Dorothy asked, looking surprised.

"Certainly!" the Scarecrow replied. "If it weren't for you, I'd still be stuck on that pole in a cornfield with no brains."

"But what about the people who live in the Emerald City?" Dorothy said. "You are their ruler now."

"I'll return when you and Toto are safely on your way home," the Scarecrow replied. "We'll start first thing in the morning."

"Thank you," Dorothy said, facing everyone. "You're the best friends I could ever hope for."

Early the next day, Dorothy packed her basket with plenty of snacks and clean clothing. We said goodbye to the green girl, who hugged each of us, including me. Then she brought us to the soldier.

"I will take you to the gate!" the soldier said as he led us outside.

The Gatekeeper gave us a friendly greeting, unlocked our glasses, and put them inside the box. He turned to the Scarecrow, and said, "You are our ruler now. You must come back as soon as possible."

*The Scarecrow is certainly getting a lot of respect around here*, I thought.

"I will," the Scarecrow said, nodding wisely.

The Gatekeeper pushed open the gate and we were on our way.

*This will be our last adventure before heading home*, I hoped.

We travelled on a flat, narrow road until we came to a dense forest. Leading the way, the Scarecrow tried to get through. But one of the tree's branches suddenly lifted him off the ground and flung him through the air. He landed back where he came from. THUD!

"Hey!" he shouted. "What's going on!"

Dorothy immediately picked up the Scarecrow and put him on his feet. "Are you okay?" she asked.

"Don't worry about me," he replied. "It doesn't hurt a bit when I get thrown about."

But when the Scarecrow attempted to walk past a different tree, the same thing happened.

"How curious," Dorothy said. "These trees don't want us to pass. I wonder if we did something to upset them."

"Let me try!" the Tin Woodman exclaimed, his axe on his shoulder.

*This fellow means business!* I thought.

Without hesitation, the Tin Woodman marched

up to the first tree that had handled the Scarecrow so roughly. When a branch tried to grab him, he quickly chopped it off.

*It's not such a good idea to get the Tin Guy mad.*

"Oh, my," Dorothy said. "That poor tree."

"Move fast!" the Tin Woodman called out.

One at a time, we scurried past the injured tree. I was the last one to go. I had almost made it through when a small branch lifted me off the ground.

I howled. I yelped. *Put me down!* I thought. *Pick on someone your own size!*

The Tin Woodman instantly arrived, carefully cut off the branch, and I was released.

*Whew,* I thought. *Thank you, old friend.*

After we went beyond the first row of trees, the other trees were well behaved and let us continue without any problems. We walked through the forest until we arrived at an open meadow.

"I see a castle!" the Scarecrow cried out, pointing straight ahead.

"We're so close to the Good Witch of the South!" Dorothy exclaimed. "I can't wait to meet her!"

# Chapter 19

# Glinda, Good Witch of the South

Our tired group finally came to a bridge. Three soldiers – all young women – stood between the castle and us. They were dressed in snappy red uniforms with gold braid.

*That's unusual,* I thought. *Most of the soldiers we've seen in Oz have been men.*

As Dorothy approached, a soldier asked, "Why have you come to the South Country?"

"To speak with the Good Witch," Dorothy replied, leaning forward to display the mark of the Good Witch of the North. "Will you take us to her?"

"I will ask Glinda if she will receive you," the soldier said, heading for the castle.

After a few minutes, the soldier came back, solemnly nodded, and brought us inside the castle. As we waited by the door, Dorothy combed her hair, the Lion shook the dust out of his mane, the Scarecrow patted his straw, and the Tin Woodman oiled his joints.

When Glinda was ready, the soldier led us to a big room. A lovely woman in a white dress was sitting upon a throne of rubies. She had thick black hair that fell over her shoulders.

"What can I do for you, my child?" Glinda asked.

Dorothy told the Good Witch about the cyclone that brought us to the Land of Oz, our adventures with the Wizard, and lots of other stuff. She even mentioned how I helped melt the Wicked Witch of the West. The Good Witch gently rubbed my head.

"My greatest wish," Dorothy continued, "is to go home to Kansas to be with my Auntie Em and Uncle Henry. They must surely think something dreadful has happened to Toto and me."

Glinda leaned forward and kissed Dorothy's forehead.

"Bless your heart," she said sweetly, "I'm sure I can tell you how to get back home."

*After so many ups and downs, that's terrific news!* I thought. *Please don't disappoint us.*

"But first," Glinda continued, "you must give me the Golden Cap."

"Of course!" Dorothy exclaimed, handing it to her. "You can use it to summon the flying monkeys three times and get three wishes."

"Yes," Glinda said, nodding. She turned to face the Scarecrow. "What will you do when Dorothy and Toto have left us?" she asked him.

"I want to return to the people of the Emerald

City," he replied, "for the Wizard of Oz has made me their ruler."

"With this Golden Cap," Glinda said, "I shall command the flying monkeys to carry you to the gates of the Emerald City."

Turning to the Tin Woodman, she asked, "What will become of you when Dorothy and Toto have gone home?"

The Tin Woodman leaned on his axe and thought for a moment. "Well, the Winkies were very kind to me," he said. "They wanted me to rule over them after the Wicked Witch of the West was destroyed. If I could return to their land, that would be wonderful."

"My second command," Glinda said, "will be that the flying monkeys carry you safely to the Land of the Winkies. I am sure you will rule them well."

Then the Good Witch looked at the Lion and asked him what he wanted to do.

"Now that I am filled with courage," the Lion said, "I would like to return to the forest where Dorothy found me. I will be the brave ruler of all the animals that live there."

"My third command to the flying monkeys," Glinda said, "will be to carry you to your forest."

The Scarecrow and the Tin Woodman and the Lion bowed their heads in appreciation.

"After those three wishes," she continued, "the power of the Golden Cap will be used up. I shall give it to the leader of the flying monkeys. He and his band will be free...forever."

*Wow!* I thought. *This Glinda seems to know what she's doing. But what about Dorothy and me?*

Dorothy must have been thinking the same thing, because she said, "You are certainly good and wise, but you have not mentioned how Toto and I will get back to Kansas."

Glinda looked at Dorothy and smiled.

"I'm sure you didn't realize it," she said, "but you could have gone back to your Auntie Em and Uncle Henry the very first day you arrived in Oz."

"But how?" Dorothy asked.

"Your silver shoes," Glinda replied. "As soon as you put them on, you had the power to travel anywhere."

*What!?! I thought. Seriously!?!*

"So I went through all of this for nothing," Dorothy said, looking heartbroken. "I can't believe it."

"But Dorothy," the Scarecrow said, "I wouldn't have received my wonderful brains if it weren't for you."

"And I wouldn't have my lovely heart," the Tin Woodman added.

"And I wouldn't be brave," declared the Lion.

"That is certainly true," Dorothy said, "and I am very glad I was helpful to you, my dear friends. But now that you have what you need, I'd really like to go home."

"All you need to do," the Good Witch said, "is to knock the heels of your shoes together three times as you make your request."

"If that is so," said Dorothy, "I will go back to Kansas at once."

# Chapter 20

# Home Again

Dorothy threw her arms around the Lion's neck and tenderly patted his big head. She kissed the Tin Woodman, who tried his best not to cry, and then hugged the Scarecrow.

"Goodbye, everybody!" Dorothy called out. "I will miss all of you very, very much!"

The Scarecrow bent over to pet me. "Farewell, Toto," he said.

I yipped to show him how glad I was to be his friend.

Dorothy held me tight, closed her eyes, and knocked the heels of her shoes together three times. "Take me home to Auntie Em and Uncle Henry!" she called out.

All of a sudden, we were whirling through the air. Everything was a blur. I could feel the wind whistling past my ears.

It was only a few seconds later when...THUD! We landed on a field of grass and rolled over three times.

"Are you all right, Toto?" Dorothy asked, reaching over to pet me.

I licked her face to show her that I was fine.

Dorothy slowly sat up and looked around. "That farmhouse doesn't look familiar," she said worriedly. "I don't know where we are, Toto."

But then she saw a familiar tree and her face lit up. "Of course!" she exclaimed. "Our house isn't here...it's back in Oz! Uncle Henry must have built this one after the cyclone!"

Dorothy bounced up and began running toward

the new house. "Come on, Toto!"

Racing behind Dorothy, I noticed that her silver shoes were gone. *They probably fell off while we were flying through the air*, I thought.

Just as Dorothy reached the front porch, Auntie Em stepped outside. "My darling child!" she cried, dropping her watering can. She held Dorothy in her arms and covered her face with lots and lots of kisses.

"Henry, Dorothy's back!" Auntie Em called out. "Toto, too!"

Uncle Henry hurried over from the barnyard and happily hugged Dorothy.

"We've missed you so much," Auntie Em said. "Where have you been?"

"The Land of Oz!" Dorothy replied. "Toto and I have had so many exciting adventures with good witches, bad witches, a talking Scarecrow, a cowardly Lion, a Tin Woodman, and an amazing Wizard!"

"We want to hear all about it," Auntie Em said as the three of them sat down on the porch swing.

Dorothy's heartwarming reunion with Auntie Em and Uncle Henry was nice to see, but I had something else on my mind. *Where's Millie?* I wondered.

I ran to the field where we chased squirrels and butterflies. No Millie! Then I trotted to the elm tree, our favorite place for afternoon naps. Nope! I didn't see my red ball with yellow dots anywhere either. *It probably got lost during the cyclone*, I thought, sadly.

I walked up to the front porch and sat down. I stared straight ahead at the nearby country road. *Maybe Millie has forgotten me. After all, I've been away for such a long time.*

A few minutes later, I thought I saw something moving in the distance. It was coming this way. *Could it be Millie?* I wondered. *Probably not.* But I kept staring. As it got closer and closer, the figure grew larger and larger. Now I could see the white and golden fur. It...was....MILLIE! And she had my red ball in her mouth! When she saw me, she dropped the ball and ran toward me.

I took off down the porch steps. After almost crashing into each other, we were finally together. We jumped! We barked! We wagged our tails! It was one of the happiest moments of my life.

"She's been coming here every day since you and Toto went away," I heard Auntie Em say to Dorothy. "Now that's a loyal friend."

Millie and I had a great time chasing each other on the grass. When we finally rested, I took a moment to look around.

It was wonderful to see Dorothy back together with Auntie Em and Uncle Henry.

It was wonderful to see Millie and my red ball.

It was wonderful to be home.

## ABOUT THE AUTHOR

Steve Metzger is the award-winning author of more than seventy children's books, including *Detective Blue* (IRA-CBC Children's Choice List), *Pluto Visits Earth!* (ABC Best Books for Children), and *This Is the House that Monsters Built*. He lives in New York City with his wife and daughter.

www.stevemetzgerbooks.com
Follow Steve on 🐦 @smetzgerbooks 📘

## ABOUT THE ILLUSTRATOR

Susan Szecsi is a classically trained illustrator from Europe. She has illustrated children's books, magazines and campaigns. Susan has an MA in English Literature and got her traditional art training at two prestigious fine art studios. Susan lives in California with her husband.

www.brainmonsters.com
Follow Susan on 🐦 @brainmonsters
or on 📷 @susan_szecsi